WED TO THE
LIONMAN

Cara Wylde was born in Romania and grew up reading fantasy novels. She later transitioned to urban fantasy and paranormal romance, maybe earlier than it was age appropriate. But don't tell her mother! She now writes paranormal romance, science fiction romance and reverse harem.

Arranged Monster Mates is a series she writes with Layla Fae and Eden Ember. These novellas follow different couples, are complete standalone stories, and can be read and enjoyed in any order.

carawylde.com

Wed to the Lionman

Arranged Monster Mates

First Digital Edition September 2023

Copyright © Cara Wylde 2023

All rights reserved.

No part of this publication may be reproduced, stored in a retrieval system, or transmitted, in any form or by any means, electronic, mechanical, photocopying, recording or otherwise without written permission from the author, except for the use of brief quotations in a book review.

This book is a work of fiction. The names, characters, places, and incidents are fictitious or have been used fictitiously, and are not to be construed as real in any way. Any resemblance to persons, living or dead, actual events, locales, or organizations is entirely coincidental.

WED TO THE LIONMAN

CARA WYLDE

Alia Terra

No one remembers the world before the Shift. It was thousands of years ago, all lost, all forgotten. Scientists and historians say that before, the world was better, brighter, and our planet belonged to us, humans. There were proud countries and bustling cities, and technology was at its highest.

We can hardly imagine all that. There is no proof, no written texts, no pictures of Alia Terra before the Shift. All we know is the face of Alia Terra now. The land haphazardly divided into territories, the walled cities, the poor living on the fringes, barely surviving.

The monsters.

The temples where young virgins can take a DNA test and be matched to one of them. An arranged marriage to a monster is often the only way a woman can save herself or give her family a chance to not starve.

This is Alia Terra. It belongs to the monsters, and we belong to them.

CAELUM

The nights were so bad that for the past few weeks, I'd been avoiding going home, and taking double shifts instead. I was working myself to the bone, and I knew that, at some point, I would collapse, but I felt like there was no other option that I could live with. Going home to an empty house was out of the question. So, I would take the second shift and the third shift of patrol, stumble home in the early hours before sunrise, crash into my bed, wake up late, have a hasty meal, then get back out there to protect the borders of our kingdom.

At first, I tried to have a normal life. Leona, the female who I'd thought was my mate, had left in the middle of the night, after two years of living under my roof and sleeping in my bed. I was hurt. No, that was an understatement. I was devastated, and I felt like I was the laugh of the lion kingdom, though those who knew me probably felt more pity than anything. It was bad either way. I tried to move on. I tried to accept the situation and forget about her, forget that she'd left me to be with a tiger shifter. But my days without her were empty, and my nights were long, sleepless, and filled with dread. The life I'd envisioned was no longer possible. So, I started doing double shifts. As a knight of the lion kingdom, I'd pledged my life to protecting our land and our king. At least this way, I felt like I was still useful to someone.

Weeks passed, and things were not getting better for me. My heart was still shattered. In a fit of despair, after drinking a few pints of ale with my friends, I decided to send my blood to the Marriage Temple the next day. If Leona could run away and mate with a tiger shifter, someone who was not of our species, then I could take a human bride.

I hadn't considered it before. I'd always believed in the purity of our race. After all, we were lion shifters – lion people, lion men – and we were strong, proud, and wealthy. It made sense to take mates who were like us and shared our values. But when Leona betrayed me and showed me that she'd never been my fated mate, something in me changed. Maybe being happy, and finding peace and love in the arms of the right partner was more important than the purity of our blood, and the purity of my future cubs.

The Marriage Temple. On Alia Terra, this was the only way a shifter, an alien, a monster, or a demon could acquire a human bride. Human females were known to be beautiful, kind, and fertile. The ones who sent their blood to the Temple for the DNA test that would match them to their perfect mate usually did it because they had no other option left. Alia Terra was all about survival. Survival of the fittest. And for human females, that was harder than for most.

After I sent my blood sample, I felt better. For a while. I had hope that the Temple would contact me soon and let me know they'd found a match for me. And then, I wouldn't have to return to an empty house anymore. There would be someone there, a human bride, waiting for me. But the weeks passed, and then a month passed, and there was no word from the Temple. I went back to doing double shifts.

Maybe I was doomed to be alone. Maybe there was no such thing as a fated mate for me. These were the thoughts running through my head, on repeat, like a mantra, as I patrolled our border with the land of the humans. The sun had just set, and the moon was high in the sky, almost full. It was a lovely night, not too warm and not too chilly, and it was quiet and uneventful. My post was at the eastern border, and here, the land of the lions was separated from the first village of the humans by a wide expanse of tall grass. Usually, the humans avoided coming too close. Incidents rarely happened. The guards and the knights on shift usually spent their time chatting and playing cards, but tonight I didn't feel like joining the others. I just wanted to be alone with my thoughts, as bleak as they were.

My light armor made no noise as I advanced over the border and into the grass field. The human village was far in the distance, and no humans roamed outside of it at this late hour, so it was safe to break the rules a little, and go for a short walk.

Sometimes I felt like I wanted to leave. Run. Leave the lion kingdom behind and try to find my luck somewhere else. But that was insane. I had the king's favor, and I was one of the wealthiest knights in the land. My house stood tall at the top of a hill, and I'd always dreamed of filling it with cubs. That had been the plan, but then Leona decided that I wasn't enough, and that the life I wanted to give her didn't suit her.

She hadn't said a word to me, so really, what I was doing every time I thought about her was to speculate. I doubted she would ever come back to tell me why she'd left, and what had been so bad and wrong in our relationship that she'd fallen in love with a tiger shifter, someone who was so different from us.

It was no use thinking about it. No use thinking about her. If she never came back, it was better that way, because I wouldn't have been able to even look at her. The magnitude of her betrayal had been too great. Unforgivable.

I advanced through the tall grass, my miserable thoughts my sole companion. I heard a shuffle ahead of me, but I ignored it. It could've been a night critter that had sensed my presence and was moving out of the way. The shuffle increased, though, until I could hear clearly that whoever it was, they weren't moving away from me, but toward me. I looked up, trying to see in the pale moonlight.

Then I heard a scream. The scream of a female. Human, for sure. She stumbled, fell, pushed herself back to her feet with a grunt. She started running again, coming closer and closer to me, but the grass was so tall and hard to navigate that she wasn't making much progress, no matter how hard she pushed.

She was running from something. Or someone. And just as I was trying to figure out what was happening, I heard male voices. Three. There were three men in pursuit of her, and they were laughing and taunting her.

"You can run, but you cannot hide," one of them said.

"We'll catch you soon enough, little bird," another said.

The third one laughed, and the sinister sound made the human female run faster.

Normally, I should've turned away and left them to their own devices. I had no idea what was going on here, and it wasn't my business. The lion people weren't supposed to interfere in the affairs of humans, unless they crossed our border. But I couldn't turn away. I was frozen in place for a moment, then I heard the female cry out as she stumbled again, and then yell when one of the men tackled her to the ground and prevented her from getting up.

"You're mine now," he said.

The hair on my nape stood on end. The way he'd said it, and the way she was clearly struggling under his weight... She didn't want him. She didn't want them, and I couldn't let them have her. Even if we belonged to different species, my principles pushed me to help her.

I could've approached them as I was, in my human form, but I didn't want them to see my face. And I didn't want them to think that they could fight me. If they saw that I was mostly human, they might attack, and that would end badly for them. I didn't want to hurt them; it was better to just scare them. So, I quickly removed my armor and my clothes, and turned.

I let the lion take over. My bones popped, my muscles rearranged themselves, and hair grew all over my body. I fell on all fours, and when the shift was complete, I craned my neck upwards and let out a mighty roar.

The human men went silent. The woman was still crying and trying to claw her way out of their grasp. If she'd heard me, she didn't care. She was too terrified, and at the moment, the three men who were trying to rip her clothes off were more dangerous to her than a lion in the night.

I pounced through the tall grass, covering the distance between me and the humans in only a few seconds. When they saw me coming, they jumped to their feet and let go of their prey. They took a step back, but they didn't turn around and didn't run. Not yet. The female crawled away, crying and whimpering, and from the way she moved, I could tell she was hurt. She tried to push herself to her feet, but she was too weak.

I jumped between her and them, and she rolled onto her back and finally looked up. The second she saw me, she went silent. She didn't move. Meanwhile, my eyes were trained on her attackers. I couldn't believe it, but they were going to stand their ground and try to fight me.

Apparently, humans weren't the brightest creatures on Alia Terra.

One of the males took out a knife and advanced toward me. The other two were armed as well, and I would've laughed, had I not been in my lion form.

Their tiny knives weren't going to help them. Not when I was as big as a horse, and much stronger than they probably imagined. Maybe they thought they were dealing with a normal lion, but they were wrong. Lions and lion shifters were different creatures, and they were going to learn that the hard way.

It was over as soon as it started. All three attacked me at once, thinking they would have the upper hand that way. I swept them off their feet with my huge paws, roared in their faces, knocked their ridiculous weapons out of their hands, and marked them with my claws. I tried not to maim them too badly. At the first sight of blood – their blood – they ran away. They stumbled through the tall grass, back to their village, whimpering like babies, though I'd barely touched them.

I turned to the female, who was still on the ground. She was breathing heavily, holding her side, looking at me with bright green eyes.

She had the most beautiful eyes I'd ever seen. On her tanned face, they looked like two jewels. Her cheeks were streaked with dirt and tears, but she was perfect to me. Her long, dark hair fell in waves down her shoulders and back, and even though she was wearing an old dress made of rough fabric, I could tell that her body was graceful and exquisite underneath.

I stepped closer and bent down to inhale her unique scent. She smelled of earth and grass, of lavender and spices. I wanted to bury my nose in her hair, but I was too close, too soon, and she shrunk away from me. I didn't want to scare her, so I stepped back. Slowly, she pushed herself to her feet, never taking her eyes off me. She walked around me, carefully, with slow moves. I could tell that she was skittish, but not frightened. She'd been more frightened by the three men, and seeing how I chased them away, she was reluctant around me, but also open and grateful in a way. I could see it in her big, green eyes.

She walked backwards, putting distance between us. I didn't move. Every muscle in my body urged me to go after her, to not let her go. There was something about her, though I couldn't put my finger on it. Something that pulled me to her, that made me want to be in her presence. I wanted to, at least, know her name, but that would've meant shifting back to my human form, and I didn't want to scare her by doing something so drastic.

When she found herself at a safe distance, she looked into my eyes, smiled, and nodded her head.

"Thank you," she whispered.

Then she turned away and started walking back to the village.

My heart did a flip in my chest, and I found myself breathing faster, like her sole presence and the sound of her voice had altered the chemistry in my body. I couldn't believe a human female could have that effect on me. Suddenly, I wasn't thinking about Leona anymore. My mind was filled with her – the woman with green eyes and dark hair. My mind played on repeat those two, breathless words – "thank you". I just wanted her to come back, so I could smell her again and listen to her voice.

But that was never going to happen.

Jade

The fright I got the night before left me sick in bed the next day. My friend, Myra, covered for me, assuring me that she could do her tasks and mine, so I could rest and recover.

Myra and I worked for one of the wealthy families in the village. We kept the house clean and helped in the kitchen, did everything that was asked of us, while being as invisible as we could. I was an orphan, but Myra wasn't. She had a family she had to take care of, so the little money she made, she gave to them, so her little brother could go to school and focus on getting an education, which was very rare if one came from one of the poor houses on the outskirts. I didn't have anyone to take care of, and no one to take care of me, so the money I made was mine. Well, except for Myra… she took care of me, like friends did, when I was sick, and in turn, I took care of her when she was sick.

As I lay in bed, listening to the familiar sounds of the house, I thought about the night before. I'd returned late, snuck in, and washed myself quickly. Inevitably, I woke Myra up, and when she saw the state I was in, she wanted to know what had happened. I cried all over again when I told her the events of the night.

The three men who'd chased me outside of the village all came from good families. We'd seen them many times at the market, and both Myra and I had noticed the way they looked at us. Especially at me. In the village, everyone knew I was all on my own. Easy prey, they'd thought. So, the day before, as I was returning late from an errand the mistress of the house had sent me on, they'd cornered me and made sure I couldn't go past them and run home. Having no other choice, I ran in the only direction that I could, and ended up trapped in the grass field, where I could barely advance without tripping.

And then he came to my rescue... The lionman.

When I saw him, I knew at once that he wasn't a normal lion. He was too big, too mighty, and his eyes were unmistakably human. He was a lion shifter from the lion kingdom, a place that I had never dared to approach before. But last night, confused and disoriented, barely able to see through my own tears, I must've gotten so close to the border with the lions that one of them had heard me.

I couldn't believe he'd come to my rescue. As far as I knew, monsters of all kinds preferred to steer clear of humans, unless they needed something from us. Like... unless they needed human brides. But even in that case, they went through the Marriage Temple, and never directly interacted with humans.

I was grateful to him. If it hadn't been for the mysterious lion warrior, God only knew what would've happened to me. Or if I'd have ever made it home in one piece. I didn't even want to think about it. It made me sick to my stomach, and I was feeling sick already. I was covered in bruises from the many falls I'd taken, but the worst part was that my heart refused to slow down, and adrenaline still coursed through my veins. I tried to sleep, but I'd only jolt awake, my chest in the grips of a panic attack.

I turned on my back and looked at the ceiling. I was going to be okay. It was over now, and the three men who'd tried to harm me the night before wouldn't dare to touch me again. Right?

I heard footsteps on the other side of the door, then a light knock. Before I could answer, the door creaked open, and the mistress of the house stepped in. She floated to my bed, sat down on the edge, and gently placed her hand on my forehead.

"You're burning up, Jade," she said.

The mistress was a nice woman. She was in charge of the house, and she kept everything under control while her husband was away with business. She had two daughters and one son, and she'd taught her children to respect the help. I was grateful to her and the way she treated me, even though I couldn't say that we were close, or that I saw her like a mother. She was good to me, to Myra and everyone who worked for her family, but she kept us at a distance, nonetheless.

"I can get back to work this instant, if you need me to," I said.

She shook her head and sighed. "That's not why I came to see you."

"Is there something wrong?"

"Yes, Jade. I'm afraid I have bad news."

My blood ran cold, and my stomach turned. I had to swallow heavily and breathe as calmly as I could to not throw up.

"The boys who gave you a hard time last night returned home wounded, their clothes ripped and covered in blood. They said it was all your fault." She looked at me with immense sadness in her eyes. "Jade, I'm afraid they might seek revenge."

Boys. She'd called them boys. They weren't boys, they were adult men who knew exactly what they were doing. I chose to keep my mouth shut. She was already doing me a favor by telling me this. After all, I was only a servant, and she had no obligation toward me.

"What do I do?" I asked. "Can you help me?"

She shook her head again. "I can't protect you, Jade. My husband is friends with their families, and I've already received word from him that when he returns, he wants to talk to you and set things straight. You know my husband. I'm afraid he won't be on your side. And I can't cross him. I'm sorry, Jade. You're a good person. You work hard, and you've been devoted to me and my children for so many years. I will pay you for this month and the next, but you can't stay. It's not safe for you to stay."

"You mean... stay here, in your house?"

"No. You can't stay in this village, Jade. You're not safe here anymore."

Tears welled up in my eyes. I tried to stop myself from crying, but there was no use. Her words crushed me.

"I have nowhere to go," I said. "Please."

She stood up. "You have to leave. I won't be able to protect you. Even if I'm the mistress of the house, I have no say in these matters."

"It's not fair," I said.

"I know. But this is the world we live in. This is Alia Terra." She walked to the door, opened it, then shot me one last glance. "Take today to rest, but you have to go tomorrow. I'll make sure you receive your pay, and I'll send Myra with tea and medicine. I'm sorry. This is all I can do for you, Jade."

"Thank you," I whispered. Because even though she couldn't do more for me, at least she was trying, and I had to be grateful.

Always grateful.

My only choice was the Temple. I'd have never thought I'd find myself in the position where I'd have to offer myself as a bride, to be taken by a monster who proved to be my perfect match. The next day, before dawn, I gathered the few personal belongings that I had, said goodbye to Myra, and took the train to the nearest Marriage Temple. Normally, women sent their blood first, so they could run a DNA test and see if they found a match. Then, a letter would come when said match was found. But I couldn't follow the protocol. I needed to get out of the village where I'd spent my whole life, and I could only hope I'd find help at the Temple.

I got there, and the Temple servants looked at me with immense pity in their eyes. It was probably my clothes – a ratty, roughspun dress, and my tattered shoes. Or maybe it was my eyes, red and puffy from so much crying. Whatever it was, I tried not to take it to heart. I hated it when people showed me pity. I didn't need it. Yes, I was an orphan, but I'd been able to make a living so far, on my own. I had my own money, and I had my honor and my pride. I'd never hurt anyone, I was a hard worker, and frankly, my only fault was that I was a woman. Alia Terra was not a place that favored women.

I approached the Temple servants, who were young women and men, and addressed them politely, telling them who I was and why I was here. One of the women, tall and blonde, with blue eyes, motioned for me to follow her inside.

"I will have to talk to the priest," she said. "We don't normally take in travelers, but maybe he'll make an exception for you."

"I'm not a mere traveler," I said. "I want to take the DNA test and see if the Temple can find a match for me. I will be a good bride, I promise."

She smiled. "Of course you will. The test is never wrong. If we find a match for you, what it means is that you and your mate were made for each other, so you will be a good bride to him, but he will also be a good husband to you."

My heart skipped a beat. Could that be true? Could that be real? Could the Temple find me someone who would take care of me, love me, and appreciate me? Even if that someone was a monster?

He could be an orc. I'd heard of women being mated to orcs. Green skin and sharp tusks. Could I live with that?

He could be a minotaur. Horns, body covered in rough fur... They were known to be farmers, and very much invested in building large families. Could I live with that?

He could be... a shifter. On Alia Terra, there were all kinds of shapeshifters. I'd met one just two nights before. The memory still sent chills through my body. Would it be so bad if I were mated to a lion shifter? Could I live with that?

"Jade?" the Temple servant snapped me out of my spiraling thoughts. "Wait here. I will find the priest and ask him."

"Okay."

I looked around me, at the high ceiling, the tall marble columns, and the altar at the other end of the room, across from me. The space was well-lit and comforting. Was it possible that I might get married in this very room? I'd never considered love or marriage before, too focused on just surviving, serving my mistress, doing good work, and flying under the radar. That had gotten me nowhere. It had gotten me here. I had yet to find out if that was a good thing or a bad thing.

When the servant girl came back, she was smiling. The priest had agreed to offer me a bed to sleep in, and three meals a day, and the payment he asked was for me to help the Temple servants. I would mostly have to work in the vegetable garden. That suited me just fine. I loved being in nature. I, of course, was supposed to let the servant girl draw blood as soon as possible, and then I was free to settle in.

Things had turned out better than I'd expected.

Three days passed. I loved it at the Temple. The food was ten times better than what the servants ate at my mistress's house. I was also given new clothes that felt soft against my skin, and my new friends cut my hair and taught me how to paint my lips red and also add red to my cheeks, to look more alive. I was a new person. A new woman. I wondered what might happen if it turned out there was no match for me, and I couldn't be anyone's bride. Would the Temple agree to let me live and work here? I didn't even want to be paid for my service. Life here was that good.

No such luck, though. On the fourth day, while I was picking vegetables for lunch, one of the Temple servants approached me, a large smile on her face. My heart dropped.

"They found a match for you," she said.

"Oh." I couldn't form words, let alone sentences. I tried not to let it show how disappointed I was.

"He will be here tomorrow, and you will be married."

I nodded.

"Aren't you happy, Jade?"

I forced a smile. "I am grateful, yes."

Always grateful.

CAELUM

As I entered the Temple, I felt my heart beating in my throat and in my head, as if it had migrated from my chest. I was breathless. In only a few minutes, I was going to meet my perfect match, my fated mate. Everyone said that the DNA test was never wrong. The human female called Jade, as the letter from the Temple had let me know, was going to be everything I'd ever wished for, and maybe more. She was going to be the mistress of my house, my heart, my life, and the mother of my cubs.

I felt the pressure of that realization. While I'd been waiting for this moment for well over a month, now I feared it to some extent. Since the night I'd saved the human female from her three attackers, my mind had clung to her image, to her deep green eyes and beautiful, flowing hair. My senses had clung to the smell of her skin and the two words she'd spoken to me. But I knew I was never going to see her again. I was here now, ready to meet my bride, and I would have to let go of her memory if I wanted to do this right and dedicate myself to the family I was going to build with the female the DNA test said was right for me.

As I advanced toward the altar, I promised myself to be present. After Leona had betrayed me, I was given a second chance at happiness. I wasn't going to self-sabotage. The priest was waiting, and I stopped before him and greeted him. He greeted me with a slight bow, then his gaze moved to a door behind me. I fought the urge to look when I heard it open, and I heard light footsteps approaching the altar.

It was her. My bride. And my heart was ready to exit through my mouth, that was how anxious I was to meet her.

She stopped at my side, and that was when I turned to look at her. I froze.

Bright green eyes and long, dark hair. She was wearing a white dress that contrasted beautifully with her tanned skin. Her lips were red and full, and her cheekbones were high and sharp, which gave her an air of regality.

It was her. Her! The woman I'd saved just a few nights before!

I couldn't believe my eyes. I couldn't believe my luck. I stood there, dumbfounded, and when she looked up at me, I realized that she didn't recognize me. How could she? She'd seen me in my lion form, and now I was in my human form, and even though my face still retained lion-like features, that wasn't enough for her to make the connection. She offered me a small smile, then glanced away, her cheeks blushing slightly. My heart skipped a few more beats, then finally settled back in my chest.

I was fine. I was more than fine. The woman who had stolen my soul with one look and two words now stood by my side, ready to be mated to me. And it struck me then. That was why I'd had to wait so long for a letter from the Temple. I'd been waiting for her, for Jade, to send a blood sample and be matched to me. It all made sense now, and it felt like divine manipulation.

The priest cleared his throat. I turned to him and saw him motioning to the golden tray in front of the altar.

"Of course," I said. "I must pay first."

I let the coins drop in the tray. The priest counted them, then looked at Jade.

"The Temple will keep the customary commission. Where would you like us to send the rest of the sum?"

"Um..." Jade seemed flustered and shy. "I don't have anyone in the world. I'm an orphan, you see."

My heart shrunk in pain at that revelation.

She didn't look at me as she continued, clearly embarrassed by her situation. "Maybe you could send it to the orphanage where I grew up? Maybe... half of it? And the other half, to my friend, Myra."

The priest nodded. "It will be done. Now, let's proceed with the ceremony."

I wanted to draw her in my arms and hug her tightly, kiss her tenderly, and tell her she was not alone in the world anymore. She had me, and I was going to take care of her, provide for her, and protect her with my life. But I couldn't do that. Not yet. She didn't even know who I was.

As the priest said the words that would bond us forever, my mind was going in circles. Should I tell her I was the one who'd saved her a few nights ago? For some reason, I felt like what I'd done then had made her send her blood to the Temple. It seemed like the two things were connected. What would she think of me if I told her? Would she thank me again? Would she be frightened? Of course, she knew I was a lion shifter. My facial features were unmistakable, and my long, blond hair that framed my face like a mane easily gave my nature away. I was dying to know what she thought of me.

As the priest ended the ceremony, I decided to keep silent. I would tell her when the time was right. Maybe she would figure it out on her own by then.

"You are now bonded as husband and wife," the priest said. "You may kiss, if you feel so inclined. Since this is the very first time you see each other, and this is an arranged marriage, I will leave it to you. The traditions of the humans and the lion people are different, but I do hope you will find common ground soon, and that you will come to love and appreciate each other. The DNA test is never wrong, but even so, it's up to you to form a connection and make this work."

I gave the priest a nod and turned to my bride. She turned to me, too, her beautiful green eyes staring into mine. Now I knew why her name was Jade. I took her hands in mine, and felt how small and frail they were, and how her fingers trembled lightly. She didn't pull away, even though I could tell she was nervous.

"Jade," I whispered. "My bride."

"Caelum."

Of course, the letter she'd received must have mentioned my name and my species. My name coming from her lips felt like honey dripping into my ears.

"I will only kiss you if you allow me to," I said.

She blushed cutely and looked away, but then took a few deep breaths and looked back into my eyes. She nodded.

"You are allowed to kiss me. After all, we're going to spend our lives together. You paid the price that was required, and I thank you for that. The orphanage and my friend, Myra, truly need those credits. I am yours now, by law, so you may kiss me."

"I want you to be mine by choice," I said. "Not now. I realize it's too soon. But at some point."

She nodded. "I am sure I will come to love you."

That made my heart grow in my chest. As for me, I loved her already. I'd fallen in love with her that night, when I'd saved her honor, and possibly her life. I'd been thinking about her ever since, and if I didn't know better, I would've even believed that I'd manifested her. But it was simple science. The DNA test. It was marked in our blood – the fact that we belonged together.

I pulled her closer to me, and she followed my lead easily. I leaned in, and she lifted herself on her tiptoes. She was so tiny compared to the females of my species that her head barely reached my sternum. She was so frail that I made a mental note I would have to be careful at all times. I could easily hurt her without meaning to. I would have to rein in my passion for her.

I saw her eyes flutter shut as we moved closer and closer, and I could feel her breath on my lips as I leaned in even more, my own eyes closing. I pressed my lips to her in a chaste kiss, and we stayed like that for a moment. It was intimate and special, and even though desire grew inside me, and the lion stirred underneath my skin, urging me to claim her, I held back, pushed my lust down, told the beast he would have to wait.

Jade was mine. By law. As she'd said. Both my beast and I would have to wait for her to be ready to become mine because she chose to. Until then, this kiss would have to be enough. And the fact that I could touch her and have her close to me would have to be enough, too.

I pulled away, and when she opened her eyes and looked at me, I saw that she was more relaxed. She wasn't afraid of me. Even more, as I turned to the priest and asked him to lead us to the portal through which I could reach the lion kingdom, Jade didn't let go of my hand.

"I have some things I need to take with me," she said. "Just some clothes and personal belongings."

I lifted her hand to my lips and planted a kiss on her knuckles. "Anything you need, my bride."

She went to fetch her bag, and I waited for her. When she returned, I took it from her. It was so light, I couldn't believe her entire life was in there.

"Have you ever traveled through a portal before?" I asked her as we both followed the priest.

"No."

I could feel that she was a little scared. Just a few moments before, the kiss had calmed her down, but now her anxiety was spiking again. It was only natural. These were all new things.

"I will hold your hand and never let go," I assured her. "It will be over in seconds, and then you will get to see your new home."

She gave me a smile, and I squeezed her hand.

This was going to be perfect.

JADE

A lion shifter! Who would've thought? When I first saw Caelum, my mind immediately went to the lion who'd saved me. And who'd also forced me to seek refuge at the Temple. But there were many who belonged to this species, and even though I'd never seen the lion kingdom with my own eyes before today, I knew it was big enough that the lion who'd come to my rescue could've been anyone.

Caelum had deep blue eyes, and long, blond hair, so soft and rich that I wanted to run my fingers through it. His features were lion-like, especially the nose, and his full lips, cat-like and tempting, especially when he smiled. He was covered from head to toe in light, shiny armor that he wore over a tunic and tight pants that were tucked in sturdy leather boots. I couldn't see much of his body, but I could tell from his exposed wrists that his skin was covered in soft hair, fur-like, as yellow as the one on his head. His hands were big and strong, and when he held mine, I felt at ease.

I was so absorbed by his presence that I could barely pay attention to what was happening around me. We went through the portal, which made me feel slightly nauseated, then we found ourselves in a large room, in a building with no windows. He led me out of it, telling me his home was not far, just up on the hill. I followed him diligently. We passed many people as we made our way to his house, and most of them were in their human forms. But I saw a few lions, too, as big as horses, and I couldn't help looking more closely at them, trying to see if I might recognize the lion who'd saved me.

"Am I the only human here?" I asked.

"Yes. Lion shifters believe in the purity of the species. I'm the first one to seek a bride from outside of the kingdom."

I didn't know what to say to that. Frankly, it felt overwhelming. I could feel the pressure to be perfect, to prove to him – and to all of them – that I was worthy, and that my genes wouldn't affect the purity of their blood.

"Why did you?" I asked. "I mean, why did you seek a human bride?"

I saw him tighten his jaw. He was silent for a moment, then said, "I'd rather not talk about it. One day, but not today." And I knew I'd touched a sensitive topic. I made a mental note to avoid it in the future. I was curious, of course, but the last thing I wanted was to pry.

The house came into view, and my eyes widened at the sight of it. It was a mansion! Three stories high, plus an attic, and surrounded by the most beautiful gardens I'd ever seen. Caelum led me to the front door, which was tall and arched beautifully, and I saw that two women were waiting for us. They smiled and greeted me with a synchronized bow. I didn't know how to react to that, so I waved, and then felt silly for doing it.

"Orla, Zura," Caelum said, "This is my bride, Jade. I wish for you to welcome her properly, as she is the mistress of the house now, and show her around."

"Of course, master," one of them said. She then turned to me, a bright smile on her face. She had the leonine features I was already getting accustomed to seeing all around me. "I am Orla, my mistress. I am the cook. If you want me to prepare any meal you love or miss from home, just come to me. I will do my best with what I have in the kitchen, and what we have in the garden."

"Thank you," I said. Honestly, though, I couldn't think of a meal I missed. I was sure what she cooked for Caelum was a hundred times better than anything I'd eaten in my life.

"And I am Zura, my mistress," the other one said. She was slimmer than Orla, but just as tall and strong. "I am the maid. Anything you need, just call me."

"Okay, I will."

Caelum turned to me and lifted both my hands to his lips. "I must leave you now, Jade. My shift starts in a few minutes. I will be home for dinner."

I didn't have time to say anything. He turned on his heel and started walking back down the hill, leaving me with Orla and Zura. The moment he was gone, I felt the atmosphere shift. Both women exhaled, their shoulders relaxing. Zura grabbed my bag and motioned for me to follow them inside.

"We are so glad you're here, mistress," Zura said.

"Please call me Jade."

She shot me a reluctant look, then exchanged a glance with Orla. Orla nodded.

"Maybe just when the master is away," she said. "In his presence, it's better that we call you mistress."

"I'd rather you always call me Jade," I chuckled. "Mistress is just... so strange. And it doesn't fit me at all. Just a few days ago, I had a mistress of my own. I was a maid, you see."

The women smiled, and I sensed indulgence in their demeanor. I blushed. I felt so out of place in my new position... I almost felt silly.

"You're not a maid anymore," Zura said. "That is my job, and please don't try to steal it from me." She winked and laughed.

That helped disperse the awkwardness in the air. I laughed, too.

"Are you hungry?" Orla asked. "You must be hungry." She looked me up and down. "Look at you! Underfed, if I say so myself. Come, I'll show you the kitchen."

While Zura took my bag to the second floor, I followed Orla into the kitchen.

Caelum's mansion was incredible. I didn't know where to look! At the beautiful tapestries on the walls, at the tall windows, guarded by heavy drapes, or at the massive furniture that was sculpted in intricate ways. Everything looked like it had cost a fortune. And Orla's kitchen was three times bigger than the kitchen in my former mistress's house. Compared to Caelum's home, all the wealthy houses in my village looked like a joke. This was true wealth, and it was taking my breath away.

Orla sat me down at the table and proceeded to heat some food for me. Soon, plates with rare steak, steamed vegetables, and warm bread were placed before me. Zura joined us, and as I ate, marveling at each bite I took, the two women filled me in. They were chatty, loved to make jokes, and I felt like they were genuinely happy I was here.

"You probably think the house needs more servants," Zura said. "You would be right. But Master Caelum likes to keep things simple. Lately, he's barely around, so I don't even have to pick up after him. I just make sure the furniture is spotless, and the carpets are clean. Aside from that, it's like no one even lives here."

Orla shook her head. "A shame, really. He rarely eats at home, so I don't even have someone to cook for. I mostly cook for Zura and myself. Since that snake of a woman, Leona, left him, he's been a shadow. Working overtime, coming home only to sleep and nibble at his food, then going back on patrol."

"That's why we're so happy you're here, Jade," Zura said. "Things will be different now. So different! You will bring joy to him and to this house."

"Sorry, who is Leona?"

Orla covered her mouth with her hand briefly. She looked at Zura. "Oh my, did I really say her name? Me and my big mouth!"

"Pff," Zura waved her off. "So what? It's better that Jade knows about her. It's no secret, anyway. Everyone knows how awful Leona was to Master Caelum."

"Awful? What did she do?" I asked. I was dying of curiosity now. Maybe Leona was the reason Caelum had opted for a human bride? It sure sounded like it.

"Master Caelum thought she was his fated mate," Zura said. "Alas, she wasn't. She ran in the middle of the night, to be with a tiger shifter, of all things! She betrayed him, broke his heart. He hasn't been the same since."

"But earlier, when he looked at you and kissed your hand," Orla said, a twinkle in her eye, "I truly felt like he was back to being himself. And he won't do a double shift today. For the first time in weeks, he will be home for dinner."

"Oh." I finished the last morsel of steak and drank a bit of water. "So, that's why he sent his blood to the Temple?" I asked. "Because this Leona left him?"

The women nodded.

"Now that I think about it," said Zura, "I'm glad things happened this way. I didn't like Leona one bit. She was so demanding, and she treated Orla and me like trash."

"So much entitlement," Orla shook her head. "Leona would've never eaten with us in the kitchen."

I smiled, wondering if inviting me to have lunch in the kitchen had been a way for them to test me. See what I was made of. From experience, I knew it was always a good idea for the mistress of the house to become friends with the help. And I felt like I was already friends with Orla and Zura.

"I'm so sorry this Leona person was such a pain," I said. "I will do better, I promise."

"You are nothing like her," Orla said. "I can tell!"

We chatted a bit more, then Zura showed me around the house. Every room we entered took my breath away. The bedroom that I was going to share with Caelum was so big that it was quite a workout to get from one end of it to the other. The bed was so large that two people could sleep in it and never find each other.

Zura proceeded to make the fire as she chatted away.

"I will always take care of everything, Jade. You don't have to lift a finger, do you hear me? Every morning, I will come and make the fire. And now, when I'm done here, I will run you a bath."

I went to look out the window. It offered an incredible view of the garden as it stretched behind the mansion. I could see rose bushes, wooden benches, and statues of lions guarding the alleys.

"Where's the gardener?" I asked.

"Oh, we don't have one. Master Caelum insists on working in the garden himself. That's where he spends all his free time. But if you ask me, we should definitely hire a gardener. Now that you're here, Master Caelum will surely be busy doing other things." She winked at me suggestively.

I looked away. I knew exactly what she was referring to. And thinking about it... that bath she'd mentioned sounded like something I needed.

She ran it for me, added scented oils to the hot water, and lit a few candles, then left me to my own devices, saying she was going to help Orla prepare dinner. Tonight was special, and they both wanted to make sure the food lived up to the expectations of the newly wedded couple.

I spent the rest of the day relaxing in the tub, amazed at how big and comfortable it was, then I took my time brushing my hair and picking a dress for dinner. When Caelum returned from his shift, I was waiting for him in the dining room. I poured him a glass of wine as he sat down, and he gently placed his hand on my arm.

"You don't have to do that. Zura can pour the wine."

"It's my pleasure, though," I said. "Plus, I wanted to talk to you before Zura came in with the food."

He furrowed his brows as I sat down in the chair next to him. He took the bottle from me and filled my glass.

"Caelum, I am very grateful for everything," I started.

"Everything? But... I haven't done anything yet."

I chuckled. "This house. It's incredible! I can't believe I live here now. So, I am grateful for that. And for your kindness and patience."

He nodded, most likely not understanding where all this was coming from.

"I just wanted you to know that I am dedicated to this. To our marriage," I said. "And I wanted to say... whatever you need from me, I will do my best to give you. That's... that's all." I was blushing again, feeling silly and out of place.

He covered my hand with his. "Jade, you don't have to do anything. You don't have to give me anything."

"But, I mean... I'm your wife."

He smiled. "And as my wife, all you have to do is... exist. As for other... duties, I can wait. I can wait for as long as you want. I want you to be ready."

Now I was beet red. I could hardly look into his eyes. I took a sip of wine, hoping it would give me courage.

"Thank you," I said.

Caelum

Those two words again, shy and sincere. "Thank you." As if I'd done anything more than my job, as if I'd fulfilled more than my duties. Now that I knew she was my fated mate, and that our destiny had always been to meet each other, I also knew that saving her that night had been my duty that I could not escape. I'd done what was right, and for that, she didn't have to thank me.

I cupped her cheek with my hand and looked deep into her eyes. "Jade, you are my bride, and my reason to be, as your mate, is to serve you."

She bit her lower lip and averted her gaze, as she always did when she felt nervous. "That means I need to serve you, too," she said. "But I'm not sure how. If you tell me, I will do it."

I smiled. "All you need to do to make me happy is to take care of the house, though Zura and Orla know their jobs well by now. You are free to manage our home as you see fit. It is yours, now, and you are free to make changes, if you want, and decorate it so it feels like home to you. Ask Zura, and she will help you."

"Okay."

"And what I hope is that you will come to love me, one day," I continued. "I want to build a family. I want to have cubs with you, but I won't pressure you, and I will not have expectations. Maybe it's better if you don't even think about it right now."

"Love," she whispered. She looked up into my eyes, furrowing her brows, as if she was taking this conversation very seriously. "Caelum, I'm afraid I don't know what love is. If I really think about it, I don't believe I've ever felt love for anyone. Or maybe I have, for my friends, like Myra, and for some of the other children I grew up with at the orphanage, but how do I know it was love that I felt when… I never felt that I was loved myself?"

"Did you never meet your parents?"

She shook her head.

I wanted to draw her in my arms and suffocate her with my adoration, but I reminded myself that it was better to take things slowly. Especially since she was being vulnerable with me right now, and I had to respect that, and not make it about myself and what I wanted to show her and make her feel. There would be plenty of time for that.

"I promise you that you know what love is," I said to her. "You know, instinctively. Trust yourself, Jade. You are pure of heart, and love will come easily to you."

"Do you really believe that?"

"I do." I leaned in and placed a kiss on her forehead. I felt her lean into my touch, and I smiled. "Let us eat," I said. "You must be starving."

As if on cue, Zura floated into the dining room and started serving dinner. My two servants were used to me by now. They could almost read my thoughts, so I wasn't surprised that Zura had sensed when she was supposed to wait, and when she was welcome to make an appearance.

"Oh, I've eaten quite well at lunch. Orla is a gifted cook."

I ignored her and piled food onto her plate, nonetheless. I filled her glass, hoping the wine would help her relax and be more open in my presence. We dined and made small talk, and I found that my heart was light around her. I was slowly rediscovering the joy of living, of sharing thoughts and experiences, of making jokes and earning laughs from someone who meant so much to me. It was better than I could've ever imagined. When I'd decided to give the Marriage Temple a shot, I most certainly hadn't expected this. I hadn't expected Jade.

She finished her meal, drank her wine, then looked at me with earning and curiosity in her eyes.

"You know... If you are willing to show me what love is, then I am willing to try," she said.

My heart skipped a beat. Jumped into my throat, more like, and I had to take a moment to swallow heavily and compose myself. I took a sip of wine and tried to calm down the beast stirring under the surface. Jade didn't know what she was doing to me by saying those words. My beast – my lion – wasn't dangerous, but he could be intense.

I stood up and offered her my hand. She took it, and once again, I felt her fingers tremble slightly. I gave her a gentle squeeze. She stood up, as well, and for a few seconds, we just looked into each other's eyes and enjoyed the energy that sizzled between our bodies. Only our hands were touching, but it was enough for me to feel the connection between us.

I wanted more.

"Jade, do you trust me?"

She nodded, but even if she trusted me, I could tell she didn't trust her voice. So, she remained silent.

I pulled her toward me and wrapped my arms around her tiny waist. She placed her hands on my broad chest, never breaking eye contact. She was so enticing that it was getting harder and harder for me to hold back the passion I felt for her. What I'd felt for Leona, even if we'd been together for two whole years, paled in comparison. I was truly convinced now that Jade had always been the one, since before I'd known of her existence – since forever.

Before she knew what was happening, I lifted her in my arms, bridal style, and she yelped, chuckled, and wrapped her arms around my neck. Her fingers got tangled in my hair, and I enjoyed how she started caressing me lightly, as if she wasn't even aware of what she was doing. The gesture felt right.

I carried her to the second floor, down the long hall, until I reached our bedroom. When she saw that I was carrying her to our bed, she blushed and hid her face in my neck. I felt her forehead pressed against my heated skin, and once again, the lion inside me stirred, impatient.

"We will take things slowly, I promise," I whispered to her. "I will be gentle."

"Okay."

I lay her down on our bed and looked at her. She was the most beautiful creature I'd ever seen. She was dressed in a long dress that I couldn't wait to peel off, and her dark hair was spread over the pillow. In the light coming from the fireplace, her eyes seemed brighter and greener.

I climbed on top of her, and she followed my every movement with interest. On all fours, I hovered over her, not touching her yet. It was intoxicating enough that I could inhale her scent and finally get drunk on it. She smelled of rose oil and grass, and there was a warmth that radiated from her body.

"May I kiss you?" I asked.

"You may do whatever you want," she said. "I am your bride, after all."

I leaned in and captured her lips in a chaste kiss. When she placed her hands on my face and pulled me closer, I growled deep in my chest and parted my lips.

She parted hers, and my tongue slipped inside. I explored her delicious mouth carefully, enjoying every second. A little moan escaped her, and the sound of it went straight to my cock. I was so hard that it had become difficult for me to think straight, and now that she was whimpering and moaning lightly, squirming under me, her hands exploring my face and my neck, her fingers threading through my hair, my cock grew even harder, so hard that it felt like was going to explode.

But I was determined to keep my promise to her. I wasn't going to do anything unless I got clear instructions from her that she was comfortable and ready.

She was a virgin, and I wanted her first time to be special, a memory that would excite her and soothe her at the same time.

JADE

I couldn't believe how gentle he was. My lust for him grew with every touch and kiss, to the point where I needed more, but didn't know how to ask for it. This was my first time with a man, and Caelum wasn't even... a man. He was a lion. Yes, he was in his human form, but the shape of his nose, his deep eyes, and the mane I loved running my fingers through reminded me that he was half monster. I had yet to see him change, and I wasn't sure I wanted to witness it so soon. This was only our first day together, and we were already taking things pretty far.

Not that I was complaining. It felt like it was all progressing naturally.

He started kissing down my neck, and I tilted my head to give him space and invite him in. A few times, I opened my mouth to speak, but no words came out. It would've been so much easier if he could read my thoughts. Though, on the other hand, my thoughts were a jumble that even I couldn't make sense of.

He started undressing me slowly, undoing the buttons of my dress and pulling it down, rolling the sleeves down my arms. The lingerie I wore underneath it was simple, yet when he saw me in just my bra and panties, he growled deeply, and I saw how his eyes darkened with desire. I got goosebumps all over my skin, and it wasn't because the room was chilly. On the contrary. It was quite warm, and his body over mine made me feel hotter and hotter.

"You are beautiful," he whispered. "I just want to touch you and kiss you all over."

"Do it," I managed to say, and I was surprised the words came out so clear and confident. I was discovering a side of myself that I hadn't known existed.

"Only because you want me to..." But I could tell that wasn't the only reason. He wanted this just as much as I wanted it, maybe more. And that sent a shiver through my body, a shiver that reached my core and made my pussy throb with something I'd never felt before.

I squirmed as my panties became wetter and wetter. I'd never touched myself down there. For one,

I'd always had to share a room with other girls, both at the orphanage and in the servants' quarters. And two, I'd never really had the time and mental space to think about my own body in that way – as a means to pleasure. This was the first time in my life when absolutely nothing was required of me, when I didn't have to work or cater to someone else's needs. The bath I'd taken earlier had been the most luxurious experience I'd ever had.

As Caelum moved down my body, his fingers tracing my curves, his lips leaving kisses and little nibbles, I was becoming more and more aware that the experience he was about to give me was going to top that.

He cupped my breasts with his big, rough hands, hands that were used to working in the garden and to wielding weapons, and that drew a sharp breath from me. My nipples became as hard as pebbles. They poked through the thin fabric of my bra, and Caelum flicked them with his fingers. I arched my back and closed my eyes as I dug my fingers into the sheets. I would've held onto him, but I was afraid I might scratch him. Not that he would've felt any pain... seeing how massive and strong he was. But I still didn't know the rules, or what I was supposed to do, so I was going to be the receiver for now and try to go with the flow.

I wanted him to remove the bra. I wanted him to take off his clothes, so there would be nothing left between us. He'd taken his armor off before he'd sat down to eat, and his tunic was light enough and loose around his neck that I could see his chest covered in blond fur. There was a scar that marked his collarbone, but it seemed to be perfectly healed.

He didn't do any of that. His clothes stayed on, and my bra stayed on, as well. Instead, he moved lower and lower, until his nose touched my pelvic bone. He inhaled deeply, and that made me blush so hard that I was tempted to pull a pillow over my face, just in case he looked up at me. Gently, he rolled my panties down my legs, and once he had them removed, thrown somewhere on the floor, he resumed his position. This time, I could feel his hot breath on my wet folds. The hair between my legs was soft and dark, and he buried his nose in it. Without meaning to, I opened my legs for him. There was no way I could have any other reaction.

Whatever Caelum was about to do to me, I needed it.

"So delicious," he whispered. Then, I felt his tongue part my pussy lips. He let out a moan of his own. "So juicy."

Now I truly had to cover my face with something. I placed my hand over my eyes, then ran it down my face until I reached my lips. He licked me again, from my entrance to my clit. Pleasure exploded within me, and I bit down into my own hand.

"Don't," he said as he reached up and removed my hand. "I want to hear you. Every whimper, every moan, every scream. I want to hear you say my name when you come."

That word... "come". I wasn't even sure what it meant. All I knew was that after it happened, I wasn't going to be the same. I nodded and grabbed onto the pillow underneath my head instead.

Caelum continued what he'd started by tracing circles around my clit. He applied different kinds of pressure, listening to the ways in which I reacted. When he pressed against a particularly good spot, somewhat to the left, I spread my legs wider, and I felt him smile against me. He'd found my weakness, and he proceeded to attack that spot with his tongue, over and over again, until I was a sweaty, quivering mess.

I couldn't hold back the sounds that erupted from my throat. As he flicked his tongue over that bundle of nerves, I felt his finger tease my entrance. He circled it with just the tip, never quite pushing in. I didn't know what to focus on – his tongue or his finger. I wanted him to do both – lick me and penetrate me – but I didn't yet have the courage to ask for it.

He pushed me further and further toward the edge, and I felt like I was about to fall into an abyss. I tried to hold back, though I couldn't say why... Maybe I was scared. Maybe I wanted to prolong the pleasure he was giving me. But at some point, it became too much. I had to let go.

The orgasm hit me with such power that when I opened my mouth to scream, his name rolled off my lips.

"Caelum!"

He didn't stop, though. He licked and pressed against that delicious spot between my legs until I started shaking and he had to hold my hips down with both hands. I missed having his finger at my entrance, but he was already giving me more than I could handle.

Slowly, I came back from the heights of my first orgasm, and my mind started to clear a little. Caelum licked me lazily, cleaning my juices until there was nothing left for him to drink. When he looked up at me, I could tell he could barely restrain himself. And I didn't want him to do it. Not for a second longer. So, I started pulling at his tunic, urging him to climb back up my body.

"Please," I said. "More."

He captured my lips in a long, heated kiss. He pressed himself against me, and I could feel the bulge in his tight pants. I reached down and tried to touch him, but he pulled away and gently grabbed my wrist.

"No."

"Why?"

"Not yet."

"Why not? I don't understand."

He sat up, and I suddenly missed the heat of his body on mine.

"I don't want this to only be physical," he said. "I will only take you and make you fully mine when I know you've fallen in love with me."

I let out a groan of frustration, which, quite frankly, surprised me. I'd had no idea I could be so demanding and impatient.

"But I need more," I tried again.

He grinned. "I know, Jade. I need more, too. So much more." He glanced between us, and I couldn't help but follow his gaze.

The tent in his pants was so big, I started to think that, maybe, he was right, and I wasn't ready. I wanted to reach out and free his cock, but at the same time, I wasn't sure I could take it. He noticed my hesitation, because he jumped off the bed and gently covered me with the duvet.

He leaned in and placed a kiss to my forehead. "I will wash and join you in bed later," he said. As he walked to the bathroom, I could tell he was feeling uncomfortable.

Had I known more about carnal things, about how the body of a man worked, maybe I could've done something to ease his pain. On the other hand, the fact that he'd just done that to me, – made me come for the first time in my life, – and he wasn't asking for anything in return, gave me a feeling of warmth and safety.

Caelum truly cared about me. I couldn't wait to sleep in his arms.

Caelum

Jade was asleep in my arms, and I couldn't take it. The warmth of her body, the softness of her skin... It was all too overwhelming. I was so hard that it was starting to hurt, my cock poking through the light pants I always wore to bed. I needed release, but I also just wanted to hold her and listen to her even breath. Nestled in my arms, tiny and frail, it felt like that was where she belonged. And I belonged with her.

But tonight was proving to be difficult. I tried to fall asleep, to no avail. The length of my cock was pressed against her round butt, and the temptation to lift her nightdress and slip inside her was too much. My blood boiled in my veins.

I needed a break from her intoxicating presence. I needed air.

Slowly, I slipped out of the bed, put on a shirt, grabbed my boots, and tiptoed out of the bedroom.

Jade must've been very tired, because she didn't even stir. Soundlessly, I climbed down the stairs and crossed the house to the door. I put my boots on, laced them up, then slipped out of the house. My intention was to go for a short walk, to clear my head and give my body a moment to calm down.

I'd never been so turned on by a woman in my life. As I started down the hill and made my way into town, stalking the quiet streets as everyone soundly slept in their beds, I wondered how I'd ever thought that my ex-girlfriend, Leona, could've been my fated mate. Two years together, and I'd never felt for her what I felt now for Jade. And I'd only known Jade for a day. Not even twenty-four hours! The connection between us was deep and undeniable. It wasn't something that I could rationalize or control, not that I wanted to. It was intense at times, almost painful, but I wouldn't have changed anything at all. Better go for a walk when it was too overwhelming than not have Jade in my life.

I slowed my pace and took a deep breath. The night was cool and pleasant, and a gentle wind made the trees rustle. The sky was peppered with stars. It smelled of pine and wildflowers. The kingdom of the lion people was rich in vegetation, green and lush. We loved to spend time in nature, and all the knights and guards I knew who lived in my neighborhood had beautiful gardens they loved to tend to. Usually, their mates were in charge of that, or they had gardeners. Some had told me they found it weird that I preferred to tend to my garden myself, but it relaxed me. Now that Jade was here, I was done with the double shifts. My time would be better spent at home, with her. I could already imagine her reading on a bench, in the shade, while I tended to the rose bushes.

I was feeling better. The walk had done its job, and now it was time to return. I already missed Jade. I wanted to have her in my arms. The fresh air had made me sleepy, and I longed for the heat of her lovely body. I started back, my pace quickening. Climbing the hill to our home was no big deal to me. I did it easily, and when I got to the top, the most I could feel was a slight strain in my calves. But that was mostly because I hadn't rested well in weeks and had pushed myself too hard with the double shifts.

A smile played on my lips as I made my way to the front door. And that was when I heard it. A scream.

Loud and shrill, and filled with terror. It was Jade. Jade was screaming.

I looked up at the windows of the second floor, then remembered our bedroom windows faced the back of the house. I heard something crash inside, like furniture, maybe, and I rushed through the front door and up the stairs.

Jade ran straight into me. She was coming from our bedroom, running down the hall while looking behind her, and she didn't see me. I caught her in my arms, and she screamed again, startled, and hit me with her tiny fists.

"It's me! Jade, it's me!"

She looked up at me, and it was as if she didn't recognize me for a minute. Then relief softened her gaze, but her body was still shaking with fright.

"Caelum! I don't know… I don't understand…"

A roar erupted from the bedroom, and Jade froze. I knew that voice. My stomach churned with revulsion, and I pushed Jade behind me.

"Go," I said.

"What? Where?"

"Downstairs. Lock yourself in the kitchen. You'll be safe there."

Because if there was one place that Leona despised and thought was beneath her, that was the kitchen. She emerged from the bedroom in her lion form, stalking me already, since she'd heard my voice and caught a whiff of my scent.

What was she doing here? What right did she think she had to barge into my house in the middle of the night and scare my bride? Yes, she'd lived under my roof for two years, but nothing that was here was hers. I'd shared everything with her. She hadn't shared anything with me. We hadn't built this place together, so she had no right to it. I realized now, as I faced her, that she'd always been more of a guest in this house, since she'd never been truly involved in our relationship and the life we shared.

So, what had made her believe that she could show up like this?

"I don't understand," Jade whispered from behind me. "What is this? Who is she? What have I ever done to her?"

"Go," I urged. "I'll take care of this."

I wondered if Jade knew. Zura and Orla had been working for me for years, and they were very good at what they did. But they also liked to gossip. It was entirely possible they'd told Jade about Leona. I should've told her first. She should've learned about my ex from me, and that was my mistake.

Jade finally complied, and I heard her rush down the stairs. That was when Leona did something I hadn't expected. She roared at me, then tried to leap past me.

I didn't have time to think. I shifted.

JADE

I'd been woken up by noises coming from downstairs. I turned on my other side, my hand looking for Caelum. He wasn't in bed with me, so I naturally assumed he was the one making the strange noises. Maybe he hadn't been able to sleep, and he'd decided to occupy himself with whatever he did when he was restless and couldn't work in his beloved garden. I yawned and buried my head in his pillow. It smelled of him, and the sweet and musky scent made me smile. I was still so tired, so I closed my eyes and tried to fall back asleep.

Then I heard footsteps down the hall. Again, I thought nothing of it. Until the door to the bedroom flew open and banged violently against the wall. I shot up in bed, trying to see in the darkness. The curtains were drawn, so there was little light. I saw two golden eyes glow eerily, and I realized they didn't belong to Caelum. Caelum had blue eyes. Whoever was standing on the threshold, staring at me, was a total stranger.

Then I heard a growl, and I realized the stranger was a woman. I gathered the sheets around me and pushed myself to the farthest corner of the bed.

"Who are you?" the woman asked.

I still couldn't see clearly. I leaned over the bedside table, feeling for the lamp switch. I pressed it, and even though the light coming from the lamp was soft and feeble, it was enough to show me who it was that was questioning me so harshly.

The woman was a lion shifter, I could tell. She had the feline features that I was getting so used to seeing everywhere.

"I'm Jade," I said. And realized how silly it sounded.

"What are you doing here, in my bed?"

"I... I don't..." I took a deep breath and tried to compose myself. She was making no sense, and I couldn't let her intimidate me. Now that I could see her face, I felt less helpless. "This is not your bed," I said.

She narrowed her eyes at me and snarled. Literally, snarled. "You're human," she said. There was disgust in her voice. "A human in my and Caelum's bed!"

And that was when it clicked. I should've known immediately, but woken up like that, taken by surprise, my brain had needed a few minutes to put two and two together. Who else could've claimed I was sleeping in her bed? In her and Caelum's bed...

"You must be Leona," I said.

"So, you know who I am."

"Yes." I dared to untangle myself from the duvet and the sheets. Carefully, I got out of the bed and stood before her, back straight, chin up. I was shaking all over and doing my best to hide it. She grinned, and I knew that she could sense my fear. Smell it, probably. She was half monster, after all. "You betrayed Caelum. Why are you back?"

She snarled again. "I will not explain myself to you." She stalked into the room, her movements graceful but dangerous. "Jade, you said. I advise you to get dressed and get out of the house. I assure you that you mean nothing to Caelum. He is mine. He's always been mine, and even though he might've spent a night or two with you, rest assured, he has no feelings for you."

I blinked. Could she be so blind? Just the fact that I was human should've been enough for her to catch up on what was happening here. It was known that the only way monsters and aliens had access to human females was through the Marriage Temple. Otherwise, we didn't mingle.

"Leona," I said carefully, "I don't think you under stand... I am Caelum's bride. We both sent our blood to the Temple, and we were matched. We're perfect mates." Her eyes darkened, and I almost took a step back, but I tried to stay strong. "This is my bed. This is my house. Because Caelum is my husband. You're the one who's not welcome here."

Well, that was the wrong thing to say. Even though it was the truth. Apparently, the truth was not something Leona appreciated being told to her face, because she let out an angry roar and shifted before my eyes.

I lost my balance and fell back onto the bed. Her clothes turned to shreds as she grew in size and her bones and muscles rearranged themselves. It looked painful, but it clearly wasn't, because it was as if she reveled in the process. When she fell on her four paws and roared once more, I could tell she felt more at ease in her lioness form than in her human form. She leaped in the air, and I rolled out of her way on autopilot. Instinct took over. I'd had no idea I could move so fast when my life was threatened.

I saw how her claws ripped the sheets, right where I'd been a moment before, and I screamed in terror as I tried to make my way out of the room. I realized that she wasn't playing around. She was determined to hurt me, if not... straight up kill me.

She blocked the door. I couldn't believe that she'd been behind me just a second before, and now she was before me, ready to pounce a second time. She was moving so quickly... It was impossible to match her speed. Of course, she was a supernatural creature, and I was a mere human.

She lunged at me, and I had the presence of mind to grab the nearest piece of furniture and throw it between us. It was a table, and it didn't do much, but Leona was taken by surprise, and she ran right into it. The wood splintered, and I had half a second to run around Leona and dash through the open door.

I slammed right into a brick wall. Okay, it wasn't a brick wall, it was just Caelum, but that was what it felt like. At first, I didn't recognize him. I was in fight-or-flight mode, adrenaline coursing through my veins, and all I knew was that I was trapped. The stairs were just there, before me, and I couldn't reach them. I hit him with my fists, but when he spoke, his voice helped clear my mind. I looked up at him, and... And I didn't know what to say.

"Who is she?"

I knew who she was, but I hadn't yet heard it from him. Was it unfair to let him believe that I had no idea what was happening and why?

"The kitchen. Lock yourself in the kitchen."

I had no choice but to listen to him. I was useless here. I couldn't help, and Leona was already out of the bedroom, even more enraged that I'd dared to hit her with a table. That I'd dared to fight her and defend myself. Though what I was doing was less fighting and more running. Nonetheless, I'd stood up for myself, and it was clear that hadn't earned me her respect.

As I rushed down the stairs, I heard Caelum shift. I couldn't help it. I needed to see. I stopped at the foot of the stairs and looked up through the bars of the railing. My jaw dropped.

He was the lion who'd saved me that night. He was the lion who'd wounded my pursuers and humiliated them so thoroughly that I'd been forced to leave my village and seek shelter at the Temple. In a way, Caelum had turned me into his bride that very night, when he'd set into motion a series of events that I couldn't avoid.

I stared at him for a moment, then he was out of view as he blocked Leona and pushed her back up the hall. I heard them struggle and roar, and then I saw them fly through the air. They started rolling down the stairs, and I bolted, running as fast as I could, not stopping until I saw myself in the kitchen. I slammed the door shut behind me and locked it, then stepped away from it and waited.

For minutes on end, I could hear the two lion shifters fight in the living room, in the dining room, down the hall... I could only imagine the destruction they left in their wake. Then silence fell, and the only thing I could hear was my own breath. I walked to the door and pressed my ear to it, trying to discern what was happening on the other side. I heard voices, and that told me the fight was over, and Caelum and Leona had shifted back. I thought it was safe enough for me to come out. I wasn't going to stay locked in the kitchen forever, was I?

I tiptoed around the mess, which was mostly broken furniture, and made my way toward the front door, where Caelum and his ex were arguing.

The first thing that shocked me was that they were both naked. I didn't know how to react to that. I covered my mouth with my hand, so as to not make a sound, and forced myself to focus on what they were saying. Of course they would be naked! Their clothes had been torn to pieces when they'd shifted, and it wasn't like they could grow them back from their very skin.

"This is not your home anymore," Caelum was yelling at Leona. "It never was, since you were never my mate. You took advantage of me, and then ran into the arms of another. Leave, and never return."

The female growled. "And the human is your mate? That's what you're saying? What about the purity of the lion blood? Have you forgotten about that?"

"I've changed since you left. I don't think that way anymore," he said. "She is my bride, and even if she weren't... Even if I never found her, I still wouldn't have taken you back. You broke my trust, and there is nothing you can do to regain it."

Leona shook her head. She saw me behind him, and her lips twisted in disgust.

"She won't make you happy," she told Caelum. "And look at her! She's so small, and skinny, and fragile that she won't even be able to carry your cubs. And I know you want cubs."

"I would never want them with you," Caelum spat out.

Also, I didn't believe I was skinny. Why did everyone insist on telling me that?

"Leave," Caelum said in a low, threatening tone.

Even though our house was at the top of the hill, it was clear that our neighbors had heard the commotion. The nearest houses had their lights on, and a few people were watching from their windows.

"Leave now," he said once more.

Finally, Leona hung her head and turned on her heel. Naked, she walked away, and I wondered if she felt humiliated. But then again, everyone who lived here was like her. Surely, they were used to seeing naked people all the time, and it was probably no embarrassment at all.

Caelum turned to me, and my eyes grew as wide as saucers. Seeing him naked for the first time was... an experience. The circumstances weren't ideal, but who cared when his body looked... like that?

Tall, strong, buff in all the right places, yet elegant and graceful... His skin was covered in the softest fur, especially his mid-section and... between his legs. As he looked at me, his cock hardened little by little, and when he closed the space between us and hugged me, he was fully hard.

"Are you okay?" he asked, kissing my forehead.

I smirked as I gently pressed myself against his thick length. "Yes. More than okay."

"I can't believe she barged in here like that and... and attacked you."

I raised an eyebrow. "How could she not? When she knows what she's lost?" I lifted myself on my toes and pressed my lips to his. I felt his cock throb against me.

"Jade..." He growled deep in his chest and pulled away to study my face again. "You're still shaking."

"Yes, but not because I'm afraid." I kissed him fiercely.

CAELUM

I knew what she meant, and I knew what she wanted. I held her in my arms and explored her mouth with my tongue. It was as if she was melting, and I was the only one who could hold her upright. She clung to me for dear life, and I loved every second of it. In that moment, she was the only one that mattered to me, and I felt deep within that she felt the same way about me. It was just us.

We kissed for minutes on end. She became more daring, and her hands started exploring my chest. She ran the tips of her fingers over my taut muscles, she caressed my scars, pulled slightly at the fur that covered my body. Then her hands moved lower and lower, until her thumb brushed the head of my cock.

That brought me back to reality. Because as much as I craved her right now, the door to our house was wide open, there were people who could probably see us, and what waited inside the house was a huge mess.

I pulled away and wrapped my hands around her wrists. She groaned as she looked up at me with lust in her eyes. I smiled and kissed her hands.

"All in due time," I whispered. "First, I need to make sure that you're okay."

"I'm okay."

"Did she hurt you?"

"No."

"I need to check." I guided her inside, and even though she rolled her eyes at me, she didn't fight me.

"Do you need me to remove my nightdress?" she asked playfully.

I should've laughed, but I couldn't. My eyes scanned the living room, and anger rose inside me when I realized that most of the furniture was destroyed – pieces I loved, some of them pieces I had built with my own hands. It was as if Leona had done it intentionally. Even though she was a strong lioness, she knew she couldn't win in a fight with me, but she'd persisted regardless. Which could only mean that she'd wanted to take revenge on me and Jade by destroying our house.

"I'm sorry," Jade said when she noticed the expression on my face.

I shook my head. "No. I'm sorry. I let this happen."

I sighed and went to look for something to throw on. I found a tunic lying around, waiting for Zura to wash it. Once I was somewhat covered, I turned to Jade.

"That was my ex," I said. She nodded, which meant that she'd known all along. I ran my hand through my messy hair. I needed to sit down, and she needed to sit down. Tonight had been taxing for both of us. The sofa had been flipped on its side, and I straightened it before motioning for Jade to sit down with me. "Leona. I assume Zura and Orla told you about her."

She bit the inside of her lip, and the gesture was so sweet that I just wanted to kiss her again. I wanted to kiss her for hours instead of having this unpleasant conversation. The last thing I wanted to talk about was Leona and the past I shared with her.

"They have," she said. "I realized who she was when she asked me to get my things and leave the house. When she said I was in her bed. I mean, hers and yours."

I closed my eyes for a second and pinched the bridge of my nose. I tried to remain calm, even though what Jade was telling me made my blood boil. What Leona had done was unforgivable. Had I been here, with Jade, none of it would've happened. But no, I'd had to take that stupid walk to clear my head of the lustful thoughts that prevented me from falling asleep with her enticing body in my arms.

"So, what happened between the two of you?" Jade asked gently.

I sighed. "Nothing. Nothing happened. She ended it. She left and didn't even tell me. I came home to an empty house. All her things were missing, and I had to learn from her brother, who lives in town, that she'd left me for a tiger shifter. Since then, I haven't heard from her. I haven't seen her until tonight. I have no idea what possessed her to come here and do something like this. I will talk to her brother in the morning. In fact, I'm pretty sure that's where she went. She has no one else in town, no other family."

"She broke your heart."

I opened my mouth, tempted to say "yes". But I changed my mind at the last moment, because it just wasn't true. Not anymore. Had I been devastated?

Yes. Disappointed? Certainly. Had her gesture made me throw myself into my work? Sure. But that was all in the past, and I realized, as I looked at Jade before me, that I wasn't the man I'd been when Leona had left me. I was someone else entirely, and the man I was now didn't suffer from a broken heart. In fact, my heart was full. It was full of Jade and the future we were going to build together.

"No," I said. "She could never break my heart, because she could never have access to it. Now I know that my heart was always meant to be yours."

Jade smiled and scooted closer. I wrapped my arms around her and placed my chin on her head. Her dark, wavy hair fell over my chest and arms, like silk.

"I know who you are," she whispered. "You saved me that night. When those three men were chasing me, wanting to do God knows what to me. It was you."

I stilled. Of course, Jade had seen me shift tonight. She'd recognized me.

"Why didn't you tell me?" she asked. "At the Temple, when you saw me. You should've told me."

"I wasn't sure it was a good idea," I admitted. "You were scared of me that night. I could see it in your eyes."

"Well, you can't blame me. It was my first encounter with a lion shifter. In his lion form. And... it was scary. What you did to those guys. I couldn't tell if you'd attacked them because they were trying to hurt me, or because they'd gotten too close to the border with your land, and after you were done with them, you would also teach me a lesson." She chuckled. "I know it sounds silly now. But I was so confused that I didn't even know where I was anymore. I could've crossed the border and not realized it."

"You were pretty far from it. On the contrary, I'd ventured a little too deep into the humans' territory. I'm glad I did. I heard you scream, I saw that you were running, I saw that you tripped, and then they were all over you. I couldn't let them..." I didn't know how to finish the sentence. It was a terrible thing to think about, and there was no point in going there, anyway. "You're mine," I said instead. "I didn't know it then. Or maybe I did, instinctively, and everything happened as fate has always meant it to happen. It doesn't matter anymore, does it?"

"You're right, it doesn't. The men you wounded returned to the village with their proverbial tails between their legs and complained to their parents. They were all from rich families. The next day, the mistress I was working for told me that I had to leave. Disappear. Because there was a good chance the three families would want to seek revenge for exposing their beloved sons to such danger."

"I'm sorry."

"It's all good. The only place where I could seek refuge was the Temple. I wasn't even sure they would take me in. I gave them my blood to run the DNA test, and for a few days, I was allowed to live with the servants and help them with chores. It wasn't a bad life, really. I liked it. I kind of didn't want the Temple to find a match for me, hoping there might be a chance for me to become a Temple servant. But then I got news that a match was found, and... well, the rest is history, right?" She laughed.

"What was your first thought when you saw me?"

She shrugged. "I thought you had kind eyes. And beautiful hair."

I laughed out loud.

"And a cute nose."

"Now you're just teasing." I squeezed her to my chest.

"What was your first thought when you saw me?" It was her turn to ask.

"I knew who you were in an instant," I said. "And it all clicked in my head. And in my heart. I knew for certain that nothing that had happened, especially with my ex leaving me, had been coincidental. It was all part of a bigger plan. I think..." I took a deep breath, inhaling her lovely scent. "I think I felt calm and trustful for the first time in my life."

"That's nice. I love that."

I pulled slightly away so I could look into her eyes. I traced her temple with my fingers and tucked a strand of hair behind her tiny ear.

"What do you say we deal with this mess tomorrow?"

"Oh God, Zura and Orla will be horrified when they come in the morning and see the state of the house."

"They will think just like I do, that all that matters is that you're okay."

She smiled. "They don't even know me that well, and they care about me. I am so grateful. For them, and for you."

"Let's get you to bed."

I took her in my arms, bridal style, and she clung to me. Avoiding the broken furniture, I carried her to our bedroom.

Our bedroom. Our bed. Jade was the only mistress of the house. And the mistress of my heart.

JADE

I barely slept. Before Leona had barged into our house and nearly destroyed it, Caelum had been the one unable to sleep. It was my turn now.

I listened to him snore softly. He had one arm underneath his head, the other over me, and he spooned me gently, giving me plenty of space to move if I needed to. The problem was that I couldn't quite move, and it wasn't because of him. I couldn't quite lie still, either. My side hurt. It hurt like hell, and I'd thought the pain would go away, but it was intensifying with every hour that passed. It was just a bruise. Before going to bed again, I'd studied it in the bathroom mirror, and even though it was large and dark, covering my ribs almost entirely, it didn't look too bad. It certainly didn't look like something over which it was worth getting alarmed.

I must have gotten the bruise when I pulled the table between me and Leona. Thinking back to that moment, my memory was jumbled. It was all a blur. It had happened quickly, and if I did get hurt in the process, probably when Leona slammed into the table, I didn't feel it. Only later, when she was gone, and Caelum was carrying me to our bedroom did I notice that something wasn't right.

The pain was dull for a while, totally manageable. But the longer I lay in bed, staring at the wall, the sharper it became. Maybe it was because I was exhausted, and I couldn't sleep. My body needed rest, so it could heal, but no matter how hard I tried, I couldn't close my eyes and just let go. It was the pain, but it was also the shot of adrenaline that I'd gotten once again after not even a week from being chased by people who wanted to harm me.

For the love of God, I could not understand why my mere existence bothered some.

Hours passed, dawn came, and light slipped into the room through cracks left by the curtains that were skewed and we'd forgotten to straighten. I felt Caelum stir beside me. He yawned, stretched, and pulled me to him. I winced silently. He kissed the back of my neck, and then started moving down my shoulder blades. I smiled, loving where this was going. Slowly, he peeled off my nightdress.

"Good morning, my beautiful bride," he whispered against my skin.

I could feel that he was hard. He pulled the duvet off us and proceeded to undress me completely. He left kissed on every inch of exposed skin, then finally, he reached my ribs and stopped in his tracks.

"Jade! You're hurt."

"Oh, it's nothing. Just a bruise."

He looked at me with knitted brows. "It's dark and tender." He brushed his fingers over it, and I tried to keep my face neutral. I really didn't want him to worry about me. "A few hours ago, you told me you're okay."

"And I am. I promise, I didn't lie, and I'm not lying. It's no big deal."

"How did it happen?"

"Honestly, I can't remember. It was all so chaotic."

"Did Leona hit you?"

"Oh, no! She didn't even touch me. I probably slammed into something when I was rushing out the door. Really, Caelum, I don't remember."

He nodded. "I believe you. Last night was insane." He leaned down and kissed me right between my breasts. "We should have a doctor look at it." He took one nipple between his lips and nibbled at it gently. I arched my back, wanting more. "I'll go bring the king's doctor. He's the best." And he made to get out of the bed. I grabbed onto him and pulled him to my other nipple. "Jade... This can be serious. We don't know."

"It's just a bruise. I don't want a doctor right now. Caelum, I want you."

He grinned and complied by sucking my nipple into his mouth. His hand slipped between my legs, and I opened them wide for him. He traced a finger between my folds, where he found me wet and ready for him. He flicked my clit as he kept sucking on my nipple and biting it teasingly. I moaned and sank my fingers into his beautiful mane.

"You need a doctor, Jade."

"Later," I begged.

His finger teased my entrance. He made to move down my body, but even though I wanted his mouth between my legs, I wanted his cock more. I wanted him inside me. I'd been craving it for hours now, and

I wasn't going to let him refuse me again. So, I pulled him back up my body and looked straight into his eyes.

"Take me," I said. "Make me yours. Now. I don't want to hear any more excuses. I just want you to fuck me, and I want you to fill me with your seed."

I couldn't believe I'd just said those words. I'd never uttered anything like it in my life. I wasn't even sure where I'd heard them, much less learned them. Growing up in an orphanage, I'd heard all kinds of things, but I'd tried to never repeat them.

This time, though, this sort of language seemed appropriate. And I could see the effect it had on Caelum. His eyes instantly darkened with lust, and he positioned himself between my legs, while being careful not to crush me under his weight.

"I will be gentle," he assured me. "I will be careful. I don't want to hurt you any more than you're already hurt."

"I'm fine," I said. "I'll be fine." I felt the head of his cock resting at my entrance, and I rolled my hips, trying to get him to move faster, push it inside me already. "Please."

When I said that I was fine, it was more to convince myself. Because the truth was that the bruise had become truly painful, and it was hard to ignore. But on the other hand, that meant that I wasn't going to notice the pain of my first time. I was feeling brave. These past few days had been intense, and they'd put me to the test. I'd survived, I'd prevailed, and I was here, in this bed, with my fated mate, with the man I was going to spend my life with, the man who was going to give me babies – or cubs, as he called them, – the man who was going to provide for me and take care of me.

I wanted nothing more than to belong to him.

"Tell me if it's too much and you need me to slow down or stop," he said.

I bit the inside of my lip and nodded. I felt him finally slip inside me, inch by delicious inch, and it hurt a bit, but it was nothing that I couldn't handle. He was halfway in already, and I felt so full. He gave me a moment to adjust as he leaned in and kissed me on the lips. Little by little, as his tongue played with mine, I relaxed. He started pushing again, until he was sheathed completely, then he stopped again.

The sensation was overwhelming. Friends had told me about their first time, and I'd tried to imagine how mine would be, but this... I'd never imagined this. For one, I'd never thought I'd lose my virginity to someone who was so... big, and thick, and... gentle.

"How does it feel?" he asked.

"Perfect," I whispered.

He smiled and started moving, ever so slightly. The pain started to subside, being replaced by pleasure. It was subtle at first, but as he thrust more deeply, as he readjusted his position and I got used to feeling him inside me, the pleasure grew until it turned me into a moaning, whimpering mess. I could feel my body turning to putty in his hands. I wanted to move my hips and meet him halfway, but I couldn't. I wanted to show him how much I liked it by contributing in some way, but it was as if my limbs didn't want to respond to the signals sent by my brain.

I clung to his wide shoulders as he increased the pace, closed my eyes, and just took every sensation as it came, letting myself be carried away by pleasure like I'd never felt before. I had no control over what was happening inside my body.

"Jade," he whispered. "You're so beautiful, so perfect..."

He was groaning and grunting above me, and when I opened my eyes, I saw that his forehead was covered in tiny beads of sweat. I realized that I was sweaty all over.

"You don't know what you're doing to me," he said.

"I... I'm not doing anything..."

He chuckled and moved faster, fucked me harder. I threw my head back and stared at the ceiling as he pushed me closer and closer to the edge. When the orgasm hit me, it was with the power of an exploding sun. I screamed and held on to him, and then, as I came down from its heights, I started chanting his name.

Caelum.

This was going to be my life from now on. These were going to be my nights. I was here for all of it.

"Jade..." He stilled, and I realized he was coming, too. He shot his seed deep inside me, right into my womb. "My bride..."

"Yes, I'm yours."

We stayed like that until he gave me every drop he had. When he rolled off me, I found that I couldn't move. I couldn't feel my body anymore, that was how intense it had been. I couldn't feel the bruise, either.

"How are you feeling?" he asked me as he gathered me in his arms.

"Mmm... I feel... I feel like I'm in Heaven."

He laughed and buried his face in my hair. "Good. Then we'll stay in Heaven for a while longer."

I knew we would have to get out of the bed at some point. Zura and Orla would want to know what the hell had happened last night. But for now... For now, all we wanted was to be with each other.

And it was a good thing I couldn't feel the bruise anymore. Maybe it was healing already.

CAELUM

Jade fell back asleep, and I snuck out of the bedroom to go downstairs and see if I could help Zura and Orla clear the mess from the night before. I found them already taking the broken furniture out and sweeping the floors. They greeted me but held their gazes down and didn't ask me anything. Which told me they'd heard all about it from the people in town.

"Jade is still sleeping," I told them. "Try to be as quiet as possible. She needs her rest."

"Of course," Zura said.

"How is she feeling?" asked Orla. "I will make her some chicken soup."

"Yes, do that. Thank you. She's shaken, but she's okay. I will go... fix this."

I put my boots on and walked out into the fresh air. It was a chilly morning, and the sky was cloudy, the sun peeking out only from time to time. By fixing this, I meant I was going to have a talk with Leona. She'd made her choice, and she couldn't just come back here, out of the blue, and expect things to be as they used to. I was mildly curious as to what had happened with the tiger shifter she'd ditched me for, but I decided it was better not to ask, lest she thought I was still interested in her and her life.

Leona's brother lived pretty far away, so I took the long walk as an opportunity to clear my head. Then I remembered with a jolt that was exactly what I'd done the night before – went for a walk – and when I got home, I found Jade running for her life. And getting seriously hurt in the process. I tried to calm my nerves. Zura and Orla were there. It was the middle of the day, and Jade was safe. She was not alone.

As the house came into view, I took a few deep breaths and cleared my throat. I walked up to the front door and knocked lightly, promising myself that I was going to keep my cool and act dignified. Leona's brother answered.

"Caelum," he said. "I thought you might drop by today."

"Stefan," I said. "Long time."

He gave me a forced smile. "Yes. I'm sorry we didn't keep in touch."

I nodded. Stefan and I had been friends before his sister had done what she'd done. After she left, I saw no point in being close with her immediate family. I knew that Stefan had always been on my side, and when Leona left me, he even told me that he didn't understand his sister at all. He was a family man himself, mated with a lioness from a neighboring town, and they had three cubs together. He'd always been the big brother who was rational and responsible, and Leona had always been his rebellious little sister. His good qualities hadn't rubbed off on her, and that wasn't his fault.

"Come on in," he said. "She's in the kitchen. I had a talk with her. She understands that what she did was wrong."

"Does she?" I tried to keep the sarcasm out of my voice, but it wasn't easy. "Sorry. It's been a rough night."

He didn't say anything and just led me into the kitchen. Leona was at the table, drinking coffee. Stefan's mate saw us. She greeted me briefly, then slipped out, saying she needed to check on the cubs.

Stefan followed her, but only after he took a hard look at both me and his sister, and made sure that we weren't going to get into a fight and destroy his kitchen.

"Have you calmed down?" I asked her.

"Yes. Sorry about the damage."

"Are you truly sorry?" I was standing, and she looked up at me. She motioned for me to sit down, but I shook my head. "You can't behave this way. You left! It was your choice. I had no say in it, because you didn't even bother to give me a heads up. What's done is done. We can't go back, do you understand that? I've moved on, found my fated mate…"

"Fated mate," she huffed.

"Yes, fated mate! Because you never were my fated mate."

"That's not why I'm amused."

"Then?"

"It's just funny to me that you believe in fated mates. Those are just children's stories."

I shook my head. "You lived with me for two years, yet you don't know me at all."

"Maybe I don't. Maybe I wasn't paying attention. You're right, I never was your fated mate. And the one I left you for never was mine."

Okay, so that made sense. It was over between them. I wasn't going to ask any questions, though. I didn't need to know details. I was over it, and I was over her drama.

"So, she is? Jade?"

Hearing Leona say her name was hard for me. Because she said it with such dismissiveness in her tone, as if Jade was just a random woman I was in lust with right now, that I would get bored of and discard soon. Leona truly could only see the world through her own eyes. She thought everyone was like her, and we were just being naïve, but we'd figure it out at some point and realize she'd always been right. This was why it was not worth prolonging this discussion.

"I'm not here to talk about Jade," I said. "In fact, the only thing I need to tell you that involves her is that I want you to apologize to her. You will come with me right now, and you will apologize."

Leona rolled her eyes and sipped her coffee. That wasn't a "no", so I took it as a "yes". Good.

"I came here to tell you that you cannot stay. You must leave town. I won't have you around Jade. You made your own bed, as they say, and this is what you get."

She sighed and stood up. "Don't worry, Caelum. I was leaving anyway. My brother doesn't want me here, you don't want me back, as you made it clear last night... There's nothing for me here. I'm leaving tomorrow. And, fine, I will apologize to your one true mate." She injected immense sarcasm into the last words. "Lead the way."

Nonetheless, this was progress. We'd talked like two adults, and now she was going to make things right. To the extent to which she could make them right. An apology wasn't enough, but it was a start. I wanted Jade to know that I cared about her, and that I was going to do everything in my power to make people like Leona understand that they needed to respect my bride, and that it didn't matter one bit that she was human.

JADE

I forced myself to get out of bed and take a bath. Zura came in to ask me if I needed help, and I sent her to bring me some water. When she returned, she found me in the tub. She'd brought me water and chicken soup, but I didn't feel hungry. I just wanted the pain to go away. The bruise was darker now, and it looked like it had even expanded, though that didn't make sense. I drank a full glass of water, thanked Zura, and told her she could go.

"I know there's a lot of work to be done today. I'm so sorry for the mess. You shouldn't have to deal with it."

"Oh, don't worry about it. Are you sure you don't need anything else?"

"I'm sure." I tried to smile, but realized it looked more like a wince. "I'll feel better in a bit. I'm just tired."

Zura nodded and left, though she did so reluctantly. I let myself relax in the hot water, hoping it would take away the pain just a little bit. My entire right side was tender, and I couldn't even stand to touch it. But there was no open wound, so I didn't understand why it was so bad. I'd slept in today, thinking more rest would do the trick and help my body heal from the inside. I probably needed even more rest. The past two weeks of my life hadn't been exactly peaceful. In fact, my life hadn't been peaceful. I really needed a break. Soon.

I lingered in the tub for an hour, but the water had become cold, and I needed to gather my strength and get out. With great effort, I pulled myself out and wrapped a towel around me. I looked at my own reflection in the mirror. My cheeks looked hollow, for some reason, and I had dark circles under my eyes. I frowned and felt stupid for not having accepted the makeup things the Temple girls had wanted to gift me. Makeup looked good on me when they applied it, but I'd told them I was helpless when it came to doing it myself, so I didn't take the powders and lip stains. Now, a bit of powder would've definitely helped, even applied clumsily. Maybe Zura could help.

I put on a light dress and went downstairs. I was impressed by how clean the living room was. It was bare, too, as the women had taken out all the broken furniture, but I was sure Caelum was going to replace it soon. Zura heard me and emerged from the dining room.

"How was your bath, Jade?" she asked. And I loved the fact that she was using my name and not calling me mistress.

"Perfect. Listen, do you have anything to cover these?" I pointed at my tired eyes.

She smiled. "Sure thing." She disappeared into the kitchen, probably to look for her bag.

I sat on the sofa, trying to find a position that was at least a little bit comfortable. I heard Zura returning, but at the same time, the front door opened, and Caelum stepped in. Zura hesitated. Behind Caelum, there was Leona, and that made Zura disappear back into the kitchen, and me stand up quickly. Too quickly for how painful my whole body felt.

Caelum rushed to me, wrapped me in his arms, and kissed my forehead. He was careful, as usual. After all, he knew about the bruise, he just didn't know how bad it had gotten in just a few hours.

"Please don't hate me for bringing her into our house," he said. "But she has to apologize to you. It will take one minute, and then she'll be out of our lives forever."

I smiled. "I don't hate you. How could I ever?" Then I looked at Leona, who was standing a few feet away, awkwardly. I could tell she didn't like seeing me and Caelum together. "So?" I encouraged her. The sooner we got this over with, the better. I understood why Caelum wanted her to apologize, but that didn't mean I felt any satisfaction. I was sure that whatever Leona was going to say to me, she wouldn't mean it.

"I'm sorry I scared you last night," she said between gritted teeth.

"Scared me? You tried to kill me!"

She almost rolled her eyes. Almost. Caelum shot her a threatening look, and she sighed.

"I wasn't going to kill you," she said. "I just wanted to frighten you, but I see how you might think my intentions were worse than that. I apologize."

We held each other's gaze for a few seconds, then I realized she wasn't going to add anything else, so I nodded.

"Apology accepted."

Neither of us meant it. She didn't care that she'd scared me, and I didn't care about her fake apology at all. But for Caelum, we were going to play our roles.

Caelum kissed my hand. "I promise you will never have to see her again."

I could certainly get behind that. As he made to escort Leona out, I sat back down on the sofa. I was feeling thirsty again. So thirsty. I touched my temple, suddenly feeling sweaty and hot, and I noticed that my skin was warm. There was a knock on the door, and that interrupted my thoughts. Who could it be? And why was today so chaotic?

Caelum went to answer, and all I could hear was another male voice. He stepped outside, closing the door behind him, and I realized he'd just left me with Leona in the living room. My senses were in high alert. I knew that Zura and Orla were in the kitchen, probably listening in, so I inhaled and exhaled deeply, trying to control my nerves. It was okay.

Leona wasn't going to do anything. And Caelum was just outside the door.

She took a step toward me, her eyes searching my face.

"You're in pain," she whispered. "Are you hurt, Jade? Poor Jade..."

"I don't know what you're talking about."

One more step, and she was close enough to reach out and feel my forehead before I could pull away. She was fast.

"Do you have a fever, Jade?"

"I really don't like the way you talk to me," I said.

Plus, she was whispering. As if she wanted to make sure neither Caelum, nor Zura and Orla could hear her.

"You're hiding it well," she said. "Better keep hiding it. Caelum is a lion shifter, after all, and our kind are known for being strong. Invincible. We don't accept weakness. Don't let him see that you're weak, or he won't respect you."

"That's nonsense."

She shrugged. "Look at what happened to me. I showed him that I was weak when I followed my stupid heart and ran into someone else's arms. Now he won't even look at me."

"I think we're talking about two different kinds of weakness."

"Look, we'll never see each other again. So, I don't care. I'm just telling you what I know. We were together for two years. You've been together for... how many days? One? Two? My brother told me he just got you from the Temple."

She made it sound like Caelum went to the Temple, picked me, paid for me, and now I was his servant. Which... wasn't far from the truth. He hadn't picked me, that was a decision the DNA test had made. And I wasn't his servant, I was his bride. But he had, indeed, paid for me.

"I know him better than you," she continued. "Caelum is proud. Do you know why he chose me? Because I was strong. Determined. Because I knew who I was, what I wanted, and how to get it. You're weak, Jade. You're... human. Maybe he doesn't realize it now, but he will one day... And who knows how he'll react? Better delay that, right? At least until he truly comes to care about you."

"He cares about me."

She rolled her eyes. "Don't tell me you believe in fated mates, too."

I swallowed heavily. Humans didn't believe in such things. In fact, I'd first heard this term from Caelum. I wasn't sure there was any point to this conversation anymore, so I stayed silent. It was a good thing, too, because Caelum said goodbye to whoever had interrupted us, and stepped back inside. He was holding a big, white envelope with a golden sigil of a lion on the front.

He looked at Leona, then at me, and he furrowed his brows.

"Everything okay?"

"Yes," Leona said, shrugging, as if she hadn't said a single word to me since he'd stepped out.

Caelum kept fixing me with his deep blue eyes, and I wondered if he could tell how horrible I was feeling. On top of the pain in my side, now I also felt like I was going to throw up.

"Jade?"

"I'm okay, don't worry about me."

Damn it. Leona had gotten into my head.

Caelum

I didn't know why, but I felt like something was wrong. Jade was hiding something from me, or at the very least, she was holding back, not feeling comfortable while Leona was around. So, I had to take care of that first.

I opened the envelope, took out the missive from the king, and handed it to my ex, so she could read it herself. I turned to Jade and explained what was happening.

"That was an emissary of the king. Word travels fast around here, even though we are far from the capital. The portals make it easy, and the king found out about what happened last night."

I'd expected that, to be fair. The king and I had known each other since before he was the king and I was one of his knights. I had his favor. Years ago, when I'd asked to be sent to a town near the border to serve, he'd tried to convince me that he needed me at his side. But the truth was that we lived in a time of peace, and the hustle and bustle of the capital had exhausted me. All I wanted was to serve my king from a place where I could find some peace and build a family.

"Leona is banished. Not from the kingdom, but from this town. She needs to leave right now, and I am to escort her, to make sure the king's wish is fulfilled."

Leona sighed as she folded the letter and slipped it back into the envelope. "You still have friends in high places, I see."

"I have people who care about me, yes," I said.

"And one of those people is the king himself. Right. You know what? It doesn't matter, does it? I've already told you I have no intention of staying. This just makes it official."

I looked at Jade for a reaction. She had her arms wrapped around herself, as if she were cold, though I could see beads of sweat on her forehead. She seemed exhausted. Maybe that was it. She just needed peace and quiet, like I did, so I totally understood.

"Jade, I will escort Leona back to her brother's house and make sure she leaves today. Is that all right?"

Jade nodded. "Yes, of course. You have to do what the king ordered."

I went to her, knelt before her, and placed my hands on her face. She was warm. Maybe too warm.

"Are you going to be okay?"

"Yes. Don't worry about me, really. I'm good."

"I'll be back soon. This won't take long, I promise."

"I can go on my own," Leona said. "You don't need to escort me."

I sighed. "The letter is very clear on that."

"Whatever you want."

She was being obnoxious on purpose. This wasn't about what I wanted; it was about doing things right. Especially since her departure affected me and my bride directly. I needed to make sure she was out of the picture, and the king knew that, and that was why he'd tasked me with carrying out his order.

I focused back on Jade. Leona really liked to distract me from her. I kissed her lips gently, and she barely responded, but I didn't make anything of it. She was just uncomfortable with my ex there.

"I'll be back," I repeated.

Jade nodded, and I took a deep breath, released it, and finally stood up and willed myself to walk away from her. She wasn't feeling well, and I needed to check that bruise of hers again, but first things first... I couldn't even follow my own thoughts when my ex's presence was so disruptive. Just her energy made me feel on edge.

"Let's go," I said, motioning for Leona to walk in front of me.

She tried to talk to me once or twice on our way to her brother's house, but I ignored her, and eventually, she fell silent. When we arrived, she turned to me and waited for me to look at her. Our gazes met, and for the first time, I saw regret in her eyes.

"I'm sorry it didn't work out," she said.

I made a noncommittal grunt.

"It was my fault. I screwed up. I hope you're happy with your human bride."

"I hope you find happiness, too," I said. "I will wait here. Go inside and grab your things."

All I wanted was to return to Jade, but an order from the king was an order from the king, and I was going to watch Leona walk out of the town. Or travel through the portal, if she so wished and had a specific place in mind. It didn't take her long, fortunately. She walked out of the house with a bag on her shoulder. Her brother gave her a hug and nodded at me.

"Let's not become total strangers," he said. "My wife and I would love to meet Jade one day."

Stefan had always been very mature and a diplomat. I appreciated that about him. Leona said she preferred to walk into the next town, since it wasn't far, and I once again let her walk in front of me. My mind wasn't with her, though. I was thinking about Jade, and all I wanted was to hold her in my arms and tell her that everything was going to be okay.

It took longer than I was comfortable with, but finally, Leona was out of the town. She wanted to hug me, but I stopped her, wished her all the best, and turned on my heel. I was feeling impatient now, so impatient that I started running. I could've shifted, but I was just as fast in my human form as in my lion form. Mostly, lion people shifted when it was needed, in battle, or when we felt like we needed to let the beast out for a bit and enjoy nature in its purest form.

I reached the house without even breaking a sweat, and I stopped for a moment in front of the door to compose myself. I smoothed down my clothes and ran a hand through my long, blond mane, then I stepped inside with a smile on my face, wanting to show Jade that our ordeal was over. From now on, only positive vibes. It was what she deserved.

When I walked into the living room, though, I saw Orla and Zura on the floor, hovering over Jade's form.

"What happened?" I ran to them, and they moved out of my way. I placed Jade's head onto my lap. She was unconscious.

"She collapsed," Zura said. "Just a few minutes ago."

"A cold compress," I told Orla. She jumped to her feet and ran into the kitchen. Then I turned to Zura. "To the castle, through the portal. Quick. Don't come back without the royal doctor."

"But I need... I need a written letter. Or at least a message."

She was right. "Pen and paper."

She brought what was needed quickly, and I wrote one sentence addressed to the doctor, and signed it. There was no time for more. As Zura dashed out the door, I took Jade into my arms and lay her down on the sofa, with a pillow under her head. She didn't wake up. I kissed her forehead, feeling that she was burning up worse than before.

"I'll take care of you," I whispered in her ear. "I love you, and I'll take care of you. I promise."

JADE

I was vaguely aware of someone leaning over me, and of a cold dampness on my forehead. My lids fluttered, and a bit of light entered my eyes, but I couldn't seem to open them completely, and I couldn't see shapes, just colors. I felt hot and drenched, but my limbs felt too weak to be able to move them and push the blanket off me. I tried to speak, but my lips didn't move. A groan rumbled from my throat, which could barely be considered communication. I heard the person hovering over me say something, their voice soft and calm, but I couldn't distinguish the words.

I fought to stay awake, to no avail. I fell into a deep sleep, and when I came back to some sort of consciousness, it was as if my body felt even heavier, more paralyzed. But at least the sounds around me sounded clearer, and I realized there were more people talking.

"Is there nothing else you can do?"

I recognized Caelum's voice, and my heart skipped a beat. Caelum. He was here. He was mine. I was mated to him. The memories of the past few days came rushing back, and I felt frightened and happy at the same time. Frightened because of Leona, happy because she was gone, and Caelum was going to focus all his attention on me. Then, a third feeling of deep apprehension snuck into my core, and it was hard for me to explain it at first. Why would I feel this way? The ordeal was over.

No. In fact, all my ordeals were over. I was still an orphan, but I wasn't alone in the world anymore. And I would never have to work for anyone, pick up after them, clean their silver, and serve their food. I wouldn't have to earn a meager living and worry about tomorrow. Then, where did this feeling of dread come from? What had triggered it?

"It's up to her to fight now," a voice that I didn't know said. "I did everything I could. She's strong. She'll wake up when she's ready."

Strong. I was strong. And that was when it dawned on me. I was strong like a human was, not like a lion. Leona had told me: lions only respected those who were strong, like them. Caelum was a lion, he was proud, a knight, and the king himself was concerned with his well-being. Was I even worthy of him? Here I was, lying on what seemed to be the sofa, unable to move my limbs or open my eyes, with people hovering over me, wondering what I was made of.

What was I made of? Flesh. Soft, vulnerable human flesh. On my best days, I could run, but not too fast. I could work, but I'd collapse in the evening. On my worst days... like today... I couldn't move.

"Thank you," Caelum said.

I heard the other man leave, and then my fractured awareness told me Caelum and I were alone in the room. My worry about what he thought of me now, seeing me like this, actually helped me return to consciousness faster. I tried to open my eyes again, and they worked. Granted I had to close them quickly because of the intense light. I groaned and covered my eyes with an arm. Which was good. It meant I could move my limbs, finally.

"My sweet Jade, I'm so sorry." Caelum jumped to his feet and rushed to turn off the lights. This time, when I opened my eyes, I could only see the warm light coming from the fireplace. "How are you feeling?" He was on the floor, on his knees, and he leaned over me as he took one of my hands into his and kissed my knuckles. "I was terrified I was going to lose you, but the doctor said it's just a fever, plus exhaustion."

"The bruise," I croaked, trying to touch my side. It seemed that I was bandaged, my whole torso immobilized.

"It's bad, but it will heal. The doctor covered it with an ointment that will help the skin heal, but there's not much he could do about it. Just don't move too much. It will heal on its own."

"Then why am I feeling so awful?"

"Exhaustion," he repeated. "You need rest, Jade. All the rest in the world, not even the slightest stress. Not until you're better."

I didn't like that I was so helpless. I pushed myself upright, and Caelum helped me sit up.

"Don't force yourself," he said.

"I'm fine. I can do it. I can sit up, I can... walk."

He frowned and shook his head. "Out of the question. I will carry you to bed, and when I'm not home, Zura will help you with everything. But don't worry, I hadn't taken a vacation in forever, and I've taken a week off now to take care of you."

I didn't know what to say to that, so I bit the inside of my lip as I felt tears stinging my eyes. I didn't want to start crying and look weaker than I already looked.

"Jade," Caelum said gently, touching my face with his fingers. My face had probably turned red from how much I was straining not to cry. "What's wrong? Tell me."

I shook my head, not trusting my voice.

"My love, you can tell me anything."

Love. My eyes widened. Well, that was new.

"Love?" I asked, timidly.

"Yes." His whole face lit up. "I love you."

"You do? Even when I'm... like this?"

"Like what?"

"Weak and helpless? Exhaustion... What even is that? Who gets a fever from exhaustion?"

For a moment, he looked at me like I'd spoken a different language that he didn't know. Then his brows knitted together, and he said in a low voice, "Did Leona say anything to you? Did she get into your head?"

Okay, so that was embarrassing. He could read me like an open book.

"It doesn't matter what she said," I tried. "It's not about that. It's just that I…"

"Shh…" He placed a finger against my lips. "Don't say another word. You are not weak, and you are not helpless. Taking care of you is an honor. Do you hear me? Please, hear me." He cupped my face with both his hands and looked straight into my eyes. "Jade, I love you. Did you know that most lion shifters don't believe in fated mates anymore? I'd almost lost hope, too. But then I saw you, that night, and I knew, deep in my heart, that our legends about fated mates have been true all along. You are the one I've been waiting for, looking for, hoping for."

I wanted to avert my gaze, but I couldn't. He had me in his grip. He held my soul in his hands.

"I… I love you, too." It was the only thing I could say.

And then the tears started flowing.

CAELUM

With rest, lots of chicken soup and cuddles, my Jade recovered quickly. I stayed by her side the entire time, and when the weather was nice, I took her outside, where she lounged with a book while I tended the garden. She loved to read, so I brought her books from the local library. That was how I learned she favored romantic novels with a dash of suspense.

We talked a lot. I told her about how I'd become friends with the king when we were just teenagers, and she told me about her friends from her previous life. She told me about her life at the orphanage, and then about getting her first job as a nanny, and her second job as a maid. She told me about her friend, Myra, and I encouraged her to write to her.

So, she started writing letters to the people she knew from before, and I loved to watch her from the other side of the room. I made sure to give her some privacy, even though I was desperate to keep an eye on her at all times. The first few days, she was weak, and I was afraid she might collapse again. But the medicine and teas the royal doctor had prepared especially for her worked, and she started growing stronger and stronger, until she got annoyed when I tried to help her get around. I wondered if I was suffocating her with my attention, but she never complained, never sent me away, never rejected me. Leona used to do that, needing a lot of space, but Jade was nothing like my ex.

"I'm grateful to have you by my side," she told me one day. "I used to feel so alone. Now I feel wanted."

"Because you are wanted," I said, kissing her lips.

Since she was back on her feet, I thought I would take her to my favorite spot, just outside of town, near the border. It was a creek in the forest, with quick, rushing water, its shore covered in grass – the perfect place for a picnic. I asked Zura and Orla to prepare a basket, then I surprised Jade in the garden, where she was just starting a new book.

"Close that and put it in here," I said, placing the basket at her feet.

She eyed me curiously. "What's in there?"

"Lunch."

"Oh?"

I started unbuttoning my shirt, which made her eyes go wide. A smile played on her lips.

"What's happening?" she asked.

"I thought I'd do something nice for you. Am I not allowed to?"

She looked around us. We were alone in the garden, but I could tell she was a bit uncomfortable. "Out here in the open?" she whispered. "I don't know, Caelum."

I laughed. "It's not what you think."

"No?" She pouted theatrically. "What a shame."

I removed my shirt, enjoying the way her eyes traveled down my torso. When I started unbuckling my belt, she cocked an eyebrow.

"I thought you could ride me," I said.

She choked on pure air. "What?"

"You know... to the picnic spot." I let my pants drop, and I removed my underwear, too. Before she could say anything, I started shifting.

"Ride you! Okay." Finally, she'd caught up with what I meant.

She closed her book and placed it in the basket, then stood up and watched me turn from man to lion. It only took a few seconds, and I was on my four paws before her, looking deep into her eyes. She reached out her hand and placed it on my snout. I leaned into her touch, and she became more daring, coming closer and petting my head. A rumble rose from my chest, like a purr. She ran her fingers through my thick mane, and the rumble truly became a deep, soothing purr.

Jade giggled as she scratched me behind the ears. "Do you like that? I'd never thought I'd own a cat. A big, scary cat that likes to purr." I let out a growl, but she wasn't impressed. She just laughed and grabbed the basket. "Okay, how do we do this?"

I lowered myself to the ground, belly flush to the damp earth. It had rained the night before, and the air was fresh and crisp. The sun was up, so by the time we'd get to the creek it would be pleasantly warm.

Jade climbed onto my back and secured the basket with one hand in front of her. With the other hand, she held tightly onto my fur.

"Go slow," she said. "I've never done this before."

Of course I was going to go slow. For one, I wasn't in a hurry. We had the whole day stretching ahead of us. And two, I loved the feel of her weight on my back. She squeezed my sides with her long, beautiful legs, and I could feel she was tense at first, but as she got used to the lazy sway of my walk as I climbed down the hill, she relaxed. When we reached the main street, I felt her squirm. I let out a purr, as to encourage her to tell me what was wrong.

"It's strange," she whispered in my ear as she slightly leaned in. "They all look at me like they've never seen a human ride a lion before." She thought for a second, then added, "Right. Because they haven't, have they? I'm the only human woman around here, and lions don't ride lions." She giggled. "Silly me."

I wanted to tell her that she wasn't silly, but that would have to wait until we reached the creek. She relaxed once more, and every time someone greeted us, she would wave at them. The lion shifters in town had gotten used to her. They'd gotten used to the idea that one of the king's knights had taken a human bride. I could only hope this acceptance would eventually turn into curiosity, and then hope and desire for fated mates of their own.

Because fated mates weren't a legend. Jade was real, and she was mine.

Arranged Monster Mates

Wed to the Ice Giant, by Layla Fae
Wed to the Minotaur, by Eden Ember
Wed to the Wolfman, by Cara Wylde
Wed to the Phoenix, by Eden Ember
Wed to the Dragon, by Cara Wylde
Wed to the Orc, by Layla Fae
Wed to the Lich, by Layla Fae
Wed to the Bullman, by Eden Ember

More paranormal romance by Cara Wylde

Grim Reaper Academy Series

Surviving Year One
Slaying Year Two
Saving Year Three
Seizing Year Four

Grim Reaper Academy Legacies

Year One: Dreamers
Year Two: Rebels
Year Three: Heroes

Printed in Dunstable, United Kingdom